8/20

Bear

and the

Oxbow Island Gang

by Rae Chalmers

illustrated by Jamie Hogan

Illustrated by Jamie Hogan

Designed and produced by:
Maine Authors Publishing
12 High Street, Thomaston, Maine
www.maineauthorspublishing.com

Printed in the United States of America

For Virginia Foster and Elinor Sullivan,
dear friends who showed me it takes courage and strength
to be your best you, no matter how old you are.

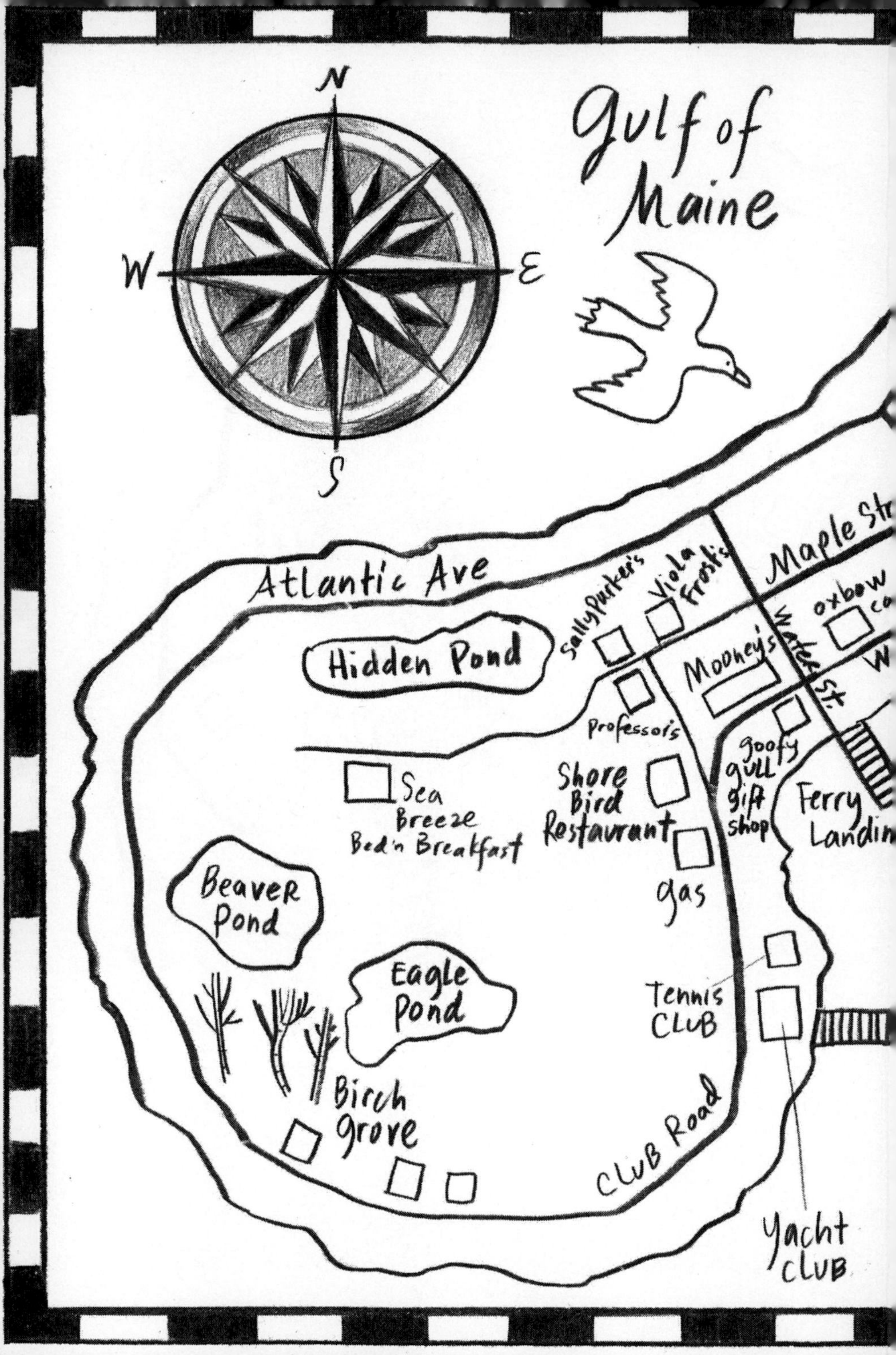
N
W
E
S
Gulf of Maine
Atlantic Ave
Maple
Hidden Pond
Sally Parker's
Viola Frost's
oxbow
Mooney's
Water St.
Professor's
goofy gull gift shop
Ferry
Sea Breeze Bed'n Breakfast
Shore Bird Restaurant
gas
Beaver Pond
Eagle Pond
Tennis CLUB
Birch grove
CLUB Road
Yacht CLUB

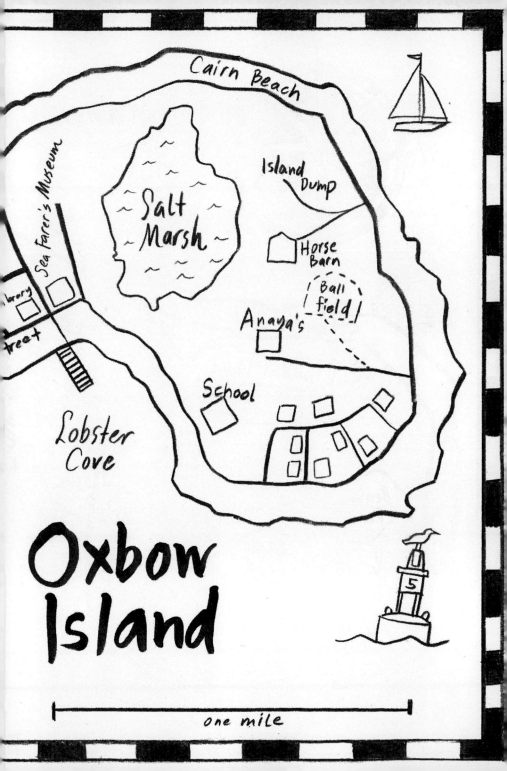

1

Eleven-year-old Bear Houtman zipped up his rain coat and pulled the hood over his brown curly hair, tightening the strings under his chubby chin. His first week of sixth grade had been a disaster. His best friend had betrayed him and he'd been kicked out of school. A crowd of joking adults surrounded Bear on this bright September afternoon. Pushing forward toward the boat-loading ramp, they all seemed eager to get home to Oxbow Island and start the weekend. With suit jackets, sweaters, and overcoats draped on their arms, they were warmed by the sunshine. But Bear was trapped in his own mood and weather: alone in a crowd, wrapped in gloom. He had to put distance between himself and what had happened. He shoved his fists deeper into his pockets and stared toward Casco Bay, waiting for the first sight of the car ferry that would take him across the water and far away from his horrible memories of middle school. Oxbow Island was the one place where people knew him and liked him.

His mother fidgeted behind him. Her coat rustled against his. He cringed and leaned toward the harbor, willing the boat to appear. Even in the jostling crowd, the people joking and sharing stories about their weekend plans, Bear could hear his mother's deep sigh. She gently placed a hand on his shoulder and he thought to himself that she had to be the most annoying person on planet Earth.

"Baby Bear," she began quietly.

Before she could utter another word, he whirled around and glared up at her. He growled, "Don't call me that."

His name was Berend, but since the day he'd come home from the hospital, most family members had settled on a nickname. Only teachers during the first weeks of school and his grandmother's elderly neighbor called him Berend. Only his mother called him Baby Bear.

"I'm sorry, honey—Bear. I know. I promised..." Her voice faded.

Bear turned his back on his mother, mumbling under his breath, "Yeah, right."

Moments later he looked up and saw the red and yellow car ferry edging around the end of the pier. His gloom lifted and a smile broke out on his face. The sight of the ferry to Oxbow Island always made him smile. "Look,

Mom, the boat's here!" It wouldn't be long now. In half an hour he'd be hugging his grandmother's golden retriever, walking in the woods or dropping his crab trap off the end of the pier. For a moment, happy island memories almost pushed sixth grade out of his mind. Everything would be better across the bay. He hoped it would. He needed that. He'd lost his best friend and the trust of his teacher and parents. But what if his grandmother was mad? No. She wouldn't be mad. She was the kind of grownup who would be disappointed. He imagined her disappointed look and turned away from the ferry, bumping into his mother.

"Bear," she began, taking a deep breath, "are you sure you want to ride the ferry alone?" Before he could answer she spoke quickly. "I know you're old enough. I'm not saying that. It's just, I'm happy to go with you. Really. I don't mind." Bear stared toward the vast Atlantic Ocean. "You've never gone by yourself before."

He was forced to step even closer to his mother as the cars drove slowly off the ferry. How many times had he ridden the ferry the three miles to Oxbow Island, his grandmother's home? At least a hundred. Still, he could feel his throat tightening at the thought of being on his own for the twenty-minute trip. Where was his boat ticket? Had he lost it already? Bear began searching his pockets while watching the people walking up the ramp following the last car.

"Bear, are you all right?"

Bear's head bobbed up and down as his hands darted in and out of all the pockets on his new rain jacket. The pockets had made the bright yellow jacket look so cool when he had selected it during their back-to-school shopping. That was when he had been excited about sixth grade and about the new rain coat. Now he hated both of them. "Yup. Yup." He muttered without looking up. There it was. He exhaled deeply and slid out the stiff blue ticket before turning it over in his hands. "Mom, I'm not a baby anymore." His voice ended on a high note that made him blush and look down, pretending to read the small print on his ticket.

A garbled voice came over the loudspeaker, mumbling jumbled words. The crowd that had been waiting patiently around Bear and his mother pushed forward. They all knew what had been announced: "We are now boarding at gate five for Oxbow Island."

Mother and son hugged quickly before Bear remembered he was mad at her and pushed away from her. "I have to go," he said and shrugged, pretending not to be nervous.

"I know." The words were barely out of her mouth before he turned and walked toward the boat ramp. "Bear!" she called.

Bear took three more steps. If she hollered "I love you, honey," he would jump into the ocean. He kept walking but turned his head and said, "Whaaat?" stretching the word to three syllables

"You forgot your suitcase." He stared at his feet and his shoulders drooped. She ran to him, pulling the suitcase behind her. "It's okay, Bear. Everything will be okay."

Halfway down the boat's metal loading ramp, as steeply angled as any playground slide, Bear hugged his mother and buried his face in her jacket, limp from a week of sixth-grade humiliation. She gently pushed him away and gripped his shoulders. "I love you." The boat's horn boomed. The captain was preparing for departure.

"Love you too." Bear grabbed the suitcase handle. With his first step it rolled heavily into his calf, shoving him down the ramp. What had his mother put in there?

When Bear recovered his balance, he saw Erin, the deckhand in charge, waiting for him. He was the last passenger, the one delaying the ferry's departure. There was no mistaking Erin's long blond braid and stern expression. She had the posture of a soldier standing at attention. In eleven years he had never seen her smile and didn't think she ever had. Some of the deckhands called him "Buddy" and high-fived him when they took his ticket. Not Erin, who was known for taking her job very seriously, especially when it came to "free-range children." That was what she called kids who played tag or had too much fun on the boat.

After he handed his ticket to her, Bear moved quickly to the boat's deck and turned to see his mother wave, blow a kiss, and send him a hug. He smiled and waved before dragging his suitcase into the port-side cabin. As the heavy door slammed behind him, Bear turned back to look through the door's window, which was gritty with salt from the ocean's spray. He could no longer see his mother or even the ferry terminal through the dirty glass. There was no turning back now. He hoped his grandmother wasn't disappointed in him. He hoped she'd let him spend his days exploring the woods and beaches with Honey the Wonder Dog. Maybe, just maybe he could then forget the embarrassment of sixth grade.

As the boat eased away from the dock, sounding its horn to signal its departure, Bear slumped against the cabin wall. Normally he would rush up to the bow of the third deck. Even in a blizzard he hurried to his favorite outside bench at the top of the boat. He was always eager to feel the wind, wanting to be the first to spot the island and all the sights along the way: seals, osprey, or a bald eagle. His mom or dad usually joined him. They always brought binoculars, but he had forgotten them in the afternoon's rush to get away from school and make the 6 o'clock boat. He didn't have binoculars, he didn't have anyone to share the sights with, and he wasn't sure he had the strength to drag his heavy suitcase up the stairs to the third deck.

The boat hit a swell and he slammed into the wall. His suitcase fell over with a crash. Several passengers turned toward him to see what had caused the commotion. Bear quickly bent over to avoid their stares and picked up his suitcase. He didn't want anyone to recognize him. His grandmother's neighbors were too friendly for the mood he was in. With his head bowed and angled away from the benches, he walked cautiously toward the front of the cabin. Anxious about stumbling and embarrassing himself again if the boat got into another rough patch, he kept his free hand out to grab the wall. The front bench was empty. Perfect, he thought, as he collapsed and felt a bead of sweat dripping from his chin. Bear unzipped his coat and slouched low on the bench, checking to see if his legs were long enough to place on the seat of the empty wheelchair in front of him.

"How's Berend?" a woman said.

Startled, Bear sat up straight, pulling his feet away from the wheelchair before turning to see Mrs. Frost.

"Oh, I didn't mean to scare you," she continued. "Your grandmother didn't tell me you were coming. Are you all right? You're flushed." Mrs. Frost slowly seated herself beside him and touched his forehead. "Oh, dear, I think you have a fever." For a moment there was deep concern in her expression, but then she patted his leg and teased, "Who's going to bake cookies for me if you're sick?"

Bear grinned at his 90-year-old friend. One of his favorite things about her was that she was even smaller and weaker than he was. Beside her he felt big and powerful.

His grandmother always described her as "a little wren of a woman." But Bear preferred to think of her as a chickadee. He took a deep breath and smelled the salt air, relaxing with the gentle roll of the boat. Maybe he really could leave his problems behind.

Suddenly their eyes widened and they said in unison, "Are you alone"—they laughed before continuing—"on the boat?" Still chuckling, they both nodded.

"This is your first time, isn't it?" Before waiting for an answer, Mrs. Frost continued, "Well, good for you." She nodded approvingly.

Mrs. Frost used to commute to work in Portland like so many of the other passengers on the boat. But that must have been twenty years ago. These days his grandmother or Mrs. Frost's daughter accompanied the elderly woman on her rare trips to the city for shopping or doctors' appointments. He didn't say, "Shouldn't somebody be with you?" but he was thinking it and turned back toward the other passengers in the cabin, looking for a familiar face.

"Nobody," she said, seeming to read his mind. "My daughter had to go somewhere so she couldn't accompany me. She helped me onto the boat. We thought we'd see someone—" Her voice trailed off as she wrinkled her forehead.

Bear tried to be reassuring. "You saw me?" But his voice broke and it sounded like a question. His heart ached as he studied her worried expression.

She smiled faintly and patted his knee as they sat there quietly. Her lips moved side to side. The wrinkles between her eyes repeatedly scrunched and relaxed. Bear waited, but she remained silent.

He turned and looked back again. There were several unattended bags a few benches behind them. "Did you go shopping?" he asked, proud at having figured out Mrs. Frost's dilemma. She must be worried about making it from the boat to the taxi with her groceries. To make matters worse it would be a steep climb up the ramp at low tide. How many times had his grandmother told him, "Mrs. Frost is too proud to ever ask for help. I have to figure out what she needs and then suggest it"? As her words floated through his head, he realized that was what he would have to do. "I can carry your groceries," Bear offered.

Mrs. Frost used her wooden cane to point toward his suitcase. He had forgotten it again. Silently scolding himself, he realized he would have walked off the boat with Mrs. Frost and her groceries and left his belongings behind. He sullenly kicked at the boat's wheelchair until he realized that could solve all their problems. "Mrs. Frost, the wheelchair. We can use the wheelchair," he said eagerly.

The look on the sweet woman's face would have been funny if she hadn't been hissing, "I will be dead before anyone sees me getting on or off the boat in a wheelchair."

Bear stifled a giggle. "Not you. Your groceries. We can put your groceries on the wheelchair. I know you can walk."

Mrs. Frost sat up straight grinning with both hands on top of her cane. Before she could say a word Bear had taken the wheelchair and filled the seat with her groceries. The bags contained the items that the island's small grocery store didn't carry: fresh berries, crossword puzzle books, her favorite shampoo, special coffee, a bag of butterscotch candies, and other small luxuries. When Bear returned to Mrs. Frost with her "necessities," as she called them, carefully loaded onto the wheelchair, they bumped their fists together, waggled their fingers, and said, "Kaboom!" just as Bear had taught her that summer.

Before he could settle into the space next to Mrs. Frost, they both noticed the suitcase again. He couldn't push the wheelchair and pull the suitcase up the ramp. Bear turned to Mrs. Frost, hoping to hear a solution. Instead, she pulled her face into a tight scowl, mouth pursed and pointing left while her nose tilted right. Her eyebrows practically met, forcing her wrinkles into an accordion. There were no answers written in the many lines that etched her face. Bear looked down, embarrassed by their shared helplessness. Would they just ride back and forth on the boat until Erin, the deckhand, noticed them? Would she order them off the boat? Mrs. Frost began tapping her cane against the boat's metal deck and Bear felt his body gently, sadly, rock along with the rhythm. The gloom, failure, and utter humiliation of sixth grade were chasing him across the ocean. He leaned toward her and their shoulders touched in shared misery.

"Good evening, Mr. Bear!" A booming voice pulled them from their isolating gloom.

Bear looked up at the tall, clumsy man looming over them. "Hi, Professor," he mumbled.

"Couldn't help but notice you running around with that wheelchair. You know how the deckhands are: 'That's not a toy, children,'" the Professor said dramatically. "'Leave it for the people who need it.'"

"I wasn't playing with—" Bear began,

"No, he certainly was not." Mrs. Frost rushed to defend him.

But the Professor raised his hand and cut them both off. "I can clearly see that. But Erin is eagle-eyed, doesn't miss a thing, and we all know that she's a stickler for the rules, especially when children are involved. Given that she is the loadmaster today I thought it might be best if I pushed the wheelchair up the ramp. I do have a certain way with the ladies."

Chuckling at the thought of anyone sweet-talking Erin, Bear and Mrs. Frost relaxed with relief. Their eyes met and Mrs. Frost said, without acknowledging their dilemma, "Well, if you think it's a good idea, I suppose you could."

Within minutes, they felt the thump of the hull against the dock on Oxbow Island. The Professor stepped toward the wheelchair and prepared to disembark, but Bear and Mrs. Frost shook their heads. Bear looked to Mrs. Frost for guidance. She looked down, picking at a sticker on her cane. Years ago, she had placed that address label on her wooden cane. Did she believe someone would mail it to her if she lost it? How could she lose it if she couldn't take two steps without it? Bear watched her alternately pick and then smooth the worn sticker. He would have to take charge again. Mrs. Frost had to be the last person off the boat; she didn't want to slow anyone else, but more importantly, she worried about being jostled in the rush and excitement of islanders hurrying home. Normally Bear would have been among them, racing to see his grandmother, but today he had to make sure no one bumped into his fragile friend.

Bear turned to the Professor and said, "We'll have to wait until after the crowd. I have that big suitcase and don't want to slow anyone down."

"Of course." The Professor gave a nod and wink of acknowledgment.

When they exited the cabin, the Professor hollered across the boat's deck, "Good evening, Erin." He appeared to tip his hat but he wasn't wearing one. "Any plans for the weekend?" Before she could comment on the wheelchair, he continued. "I'll have this back on the boat before you can say Jack Robinson."

Bear waited for Erin to argue. What did that even mean, Jack Robinson? The Professor could be just plain weird at times. If Mrs. Frost hadn't needed their help, Bear would have rushed off the boat. The Professor smiled and waved at Erin as he pushed the wheelchair toward the ramp without waiting for a response.

Bear watched, expecting her to holler, "Stop!" But instead she said, "Have a good weekend."

And so they were the last people off the 6 o'clock ferry that Friday. The Professor, an exceptionally tall, middle-aged black man pushing a wheelchair full of groceries, led the way. Bear Houtman a short, round, curly haired, pale boy dragging a large suitcase, was last. Viola Frost was between them, protected, a tiny ninety-year-old gripping the ramp's railing with one hand and her wooden cane with the other. They all leaned forward, straining against the incline as they climbed the steep ramp, focused on making it to shore. They were so intent they didn't notice Bear's grandmother, Sally Parker, until she was halfway down the ramp.

"Thank you!" she said to the Professor, patting his shoulder, before dropping back to ruffle Bear's hair and whisper, "I'm proud of you for helping out, Buckaroo Bear."

Bear beamed and stood up straight. His suitcase seemed lighter as the wheels squeaked against the metal ramp.

His grandmother walked beside Mrs. Frost, one hand cupping the elderly woman's elbow, and said, "You're hanging out with an awfully rough crowd these days, Viola."

Viola Frost tilted her head toward the tall man in front of her and said, "You're telling me. Sally, that one there is a wheelchair thief."

2

Once Mrs. Frost and her packages had been placed in the island's taxi, Bear stood with his grandmother and the Professor in front of the Oxbow Café. He was torn between his excitement to be back on the island and anxiety. Before this visit, he had never come to his grandmother's for anything other than a vacation. As he watched the ferry begin its trip back to Portland, he heard the two adults talking but barely paid attention. Maybe they could get a pastry at the café in the morning. If the weather were nice tomorrow, he wanted to look for beach glass, take Honey the Wonder Dog for a long walk in the woods, and then get ice cream from the Goofy Gull Gift Shop. But what if he was grounded, placed under house arrest? What if Oxbow Island was going to be his Alcatraz? An island prison, punishment for what he had done at school, with his grandmother as jailer. She hadn't seemed mad or disappointed when she met the boat. That could change when they were alone together. Bear stepped off the sidewalk and stared at his feet, not wanting to attract her attention.

"Bear? Buckaroo Bear?"

"What? What?" he answered, and then noticed the Professor walking up the hill. "Gramma, the Professor's got my suitcase!"

He must have heard Bear, because he turned and said, "No need for concern. I'll leave it on your porch. What have you stowed in your luggage? Boulders?"

Bear shrugged. He didn't know what his mother had packed. She must have put all his textbooks in there, and that was how he would be spending his days on the island: a prison term filled with questions from the end of each chapter. He could forget about all the island activities he loved: identifying birds, looking for beavers, and building rock sculptures on the back shore. His shoulders drooped even further.

"Bear, I thought we could get a pizza from Mooney's for dinner. If we hurry, we can watch the sunset while they're making it. Should be a good show tonight with those wispy clouds on the horizon."

"Really?" Bear searched her face for evidence that she knew what he had done. The exact reason he was not allowed at school for a week. The specific details of why he hoped he never had to return to sixth grade. Was that possible? His mother must have told her but his grandmother was acting like everything was normal. "Really?" he repeated, hoping for a sign but not wanting to say anything that would change her mind about the pizza. It was probably best if he did not say anything at all. So, he took her by the hand and tugged her up the hill to the grocery store.

Anxious about what other customers or even Mike Mooney, the owner, might ask him about his visit to the island, Bear decided to avoid the store. "Why don't I save us some seats while you order the pizza?"

Whether they were sitting on the shore watching a moon rising, a sunset, a storm surge, or a sunrise, Bear and his grandmother always pretended they were in a movie theater. "These are great seats." "Better hurry before the show starts." Or, "I hope no one talks during the show." They would say these things to each other with mock seriousness.

His grandmother seemed surprised. Normally, Bear was eager to go in and see what was new in Mooney's Market. Standing in the potato chip aisle, you could guess the day of the week, time of year, and even whether a bad storm was forecast to hit the island. In summer the shelves were half empty by Monday morning. Toilet paper, bread, and other essentials were all gone by Tuesday. It was impossible to keep up with the demands of the summer crowds. On Wednesdays the shelves were restocked and the aisles were crammed with boxes making it almost impossible to push a cart through the store. Wednesday was the day all the old-timers shopped. This included his grandmother and Mrs. Frost. In the summer, Mr. Mooney would stock fancy cheeses and expensive crackers for the summer people. Half the potato chips were replaced by wines from around the world. But in winter the potato chips, dips, and canned goods returned. Cabbage filled the produce section and sparkling water was replaced by cheap brands of cola. Potatoes and onions filled in the gaps where artichokes and ginger root had been.

Bear preferred the more basic macaroni and cheese, Cheetos, and hot dogs that appeared once the summer people left in the fall. Another reason he favored the store after Labor Day was that the employees became friendlier as the weather cooled off and the crowds headed to warmer, more convenient homes. After Labor Day, shoppers were encouraged to remain after they had paid for their groceries, and they'd snack on their purchases, talking about the headlines in the newspaper or catching up on the island gossip that his grandmother was too polite to discuss at home.

Maybe tomorrow, Bear thought as he sat on the grassy slope between the Shorebird Restaurant and the gas station. There were a few other clusters of people, taking a break to chat and watch the ocean darken as the sun slid closer toward the silhouette of Portland's old brick buildings on the other side of Casco Bay. Below Bear, two little girls were shrieking as they chased each other up and down the hill. Their parents watched and leaned into each other, heads and shoulders touching. Watching the couple, Bear felt homesick, missing his parents.

"Did I miss anything?" his grandmother asked as she plopped down beside him. She gave him a quick hug. "I missed you."

Bear smiled, shook his head *no,* and they turned back toward the west, where the sun's pinks and purples were reflected on the ocean. They heard a quiet gasp from farther down the hill, followed by a giggle. The bottoms of the scattered clouds glowed pink with the reflected light.

"It's like silent fireworks," Bear whispered.

Sally Parker put her arm around her grandson's shoulders until the last rays of light were gone. "That was an excellent show!" she said as they stood up. "Let's grab that pizza and head home for dinner."

Sitting at the dining room table in his grandmother's house with Honey the Wonder Dog lying on his feet snoring quietly, Bear smiled as he reached for a piece of pizza, anticipating the taste and feel of warm cheese and salty pepperoni in his mouth. His stomach growled. His school lunch was a distant memory.

Sally Parker rested her elbows on the table, leaned forward, and said, "Want to tell me what happened?"

The pizza suddenly felt limp in his hand and he dropped it on the plate. If he looked at his grandmother, he knew that she would be able to read the expression on his face, so he stared intently at the pizza in front of him, counting the pieces of pepperoni again and again. Maybe she didn't know everything. But Bear had spent enough time around adults to know that when grownups asked you a question, they already knew the answer. The punishment depended as much on how honest you were as how bad the behavior had been. It was hard to imagine that his mother had not told his grandmother most of the details. He considered making up a story, but one glance at his grandmother's calm green eyes staring into his and the words tumbled out of his mouth from the very beginning: the last day of fifth grade.

"You know Marky my best friend? Now he calls himself Mark. We shared the best comic book collection. Honestly, he wasn't my best friend, he was my only friend. But I never minded. We even got the same home-room teacher for sixth grade, Ms. Alcott. Everyone said she was the best. It was going to be great.

"But he went away to sports camp this summer and everything changed. Marky became Mark, a cool athlete." When Bear said "athlete" it sounded like *ath-the-leeeeeet*. Bear glanced up at his grandmother. She nodded. "He was gone for practically the whole summer. He never cared about sports before but this summer he went to soccer camp, basketball camp, baseball camp, and archery camp. Archery? Do you even know what that is?"

His grandmother nodded her head and remained silent.

"Well, I didn't." Bear picked up a piece of pepperoni and ate it. "I do now, bows and arrows and targets on the side of fake deer. He never cared about hunting before either but now he's an ath-the-leeet and a big game hunter."

"That's what you fought about?"

"No. Not really. Maybe—a little bit." Bear looked across the table at the puzzled expression on his grandmother's face. "I don't want you to be mad at me."

"I won't."

"Mom and Dad are."

"I think they're concerned, not mad."

Bear thought about this for a minute. "Maybe. I have to tell the whole story. This didn't just start today or even this week."

The corners of his grandmother's mouth turned up. "Of course. I'm not going anywhere," she said as she lifted a piece of pizza to her mouth.

"We went home right after the Fourth of July," Bear said, referring to the vacation he and his parents had enjoyed on Oxbow Island. "Marky—Mark—was gone. I didn't have anyone to hang out with. I just sat in the backyard organizing my comic books, arguing with myself about who was better, Captain America or Wolverine, and practicing tying knots at the picnic table." He paused, remembering how long and boring those hot days in July had been. "These girls, Jasmine and Devi, were always playing in the yard behind ours. That's where Jasmine lives. Sometime I would spy on them, listen to them through the fence. I didn't think they'd noticed me, but one day they jumped up on the fence. They started talking. Said they wanted to build a tree house but they didn't have a tree. I thought that was pretty funny. They asked if they could borrow our tree."

"How do you borrow a fifty-year-old oak tree?"

"Exactly! That's what I said. They said they wouldn't take it. Obviously. They wanted to build the tree house in the tree in our yard and I could help if I wanted to. What else did I have to do? So we started that day, getting materials together. Our parents even helped and became friends. It's really cool and I used a lot of those knots that we learned at the Seafarers' Museum. Mom is sewing a canvas roof. It looks like a sail. And this weekend we're going to have a tree house celebration barbecue." Bear stopped talking. Until he said it, he had forgotten about the barbecue they had been planning for Saturday. Tomorrow. Would they have it without him?

"But you're here instead." His grandmother finished the thought for him. Bear remained silent so she continued slowly, "This doesn't sound like something that leads to"—she struggled for the right word—"difficulties."

"I know, right? It was fun. Honestly, by August I'd stopped missing Marky—Mark—at all."

"The first day of school, Mark and I walked there together like we always had, but before school started, we were outside just talking and these guys he'd met at summer camp walked up. They were talking about sports and kids I'd never heard of. At lunch, I went to sit with him, and this kid, Gordy, he's huge, monster-sized, said I couldn't sit there. He said the table was for guys who played soccer. I looked at Mark but he just looked away. Didn't move over to make room for me or anything." Bear remembered how embarrassed he had been, standing alone in the middle of the cafeteria, surrounded by clusters of joking friends. Everyone could see that he didn't belong. He had never been part of a group but he had always had one friend, someone to sit with and share jokes that made sense only to them.

"I walked away." Bear reached down and laid a hand on Honey's belly. His hand rose and fell with her breathing. "I was going to go to the bathroom and stay there for the rest of lunch but I saw Jasmine and Devi, waving at me. The table was all girls." Bear hoped his grandmother would keep that a secret. She nodded her head so he continued. "They moved over and made room for me. Everybody was nice. Like it was no big deal. That afternoon, they walked home from school with me, too. We had a lot of planning to do for the barbecue and last minute things to fix on the tree house so I figured it was good.

"But the next day, Mark and his new friends, Gordy and Irvin, walked by every time I was talking to Jasmine and Devi and said things like, 'How're you girls doing today?' 'You girls going shopping after school?' 'Don't want to interrupt the girl talk.' They meant me too, that I'm a girl. Jasmine and Devi told me to ignore it and I did for three days. But today I just couldn't take it anymore." Bear hung his head as he remembered how angry he had been just eight hours earlier.

"We were eating our lunches and Jasmine was making a list of what we wanted to have at the barbecue, all our favorite foods, so her mom could go grocery shopping. Mark, Gordy, and Irvin came by and Gordy grabbed the list from Jasmine and started reading it out loud. Then he said, 'Look the girls are going grocery shopping,' and on and on about us cooking. Everyone was staring at me and laughing."

"Bear, there's nothing wrong with going grocery shopping, cooking, or being a girl."

"He was making fun of me."

"Your father goes grocery shopping and is an excellent cook."

"I knew you wouldn't understand." Bear stabbed his uneaten pizza with his fork and began spinning it on the plate. It was cold and he had lost his appetite.

"I understand that they're bullies." His grandmother leaned across the table. "Maybe they should have been suspended, not you."

Bear's head snapped up when she said *suspended*. His mother had told her. "Well, I did something worse." There was no point in trying to keep anything a secret.

"Mostly it had been Gordy and Irvin saying stuff but after lunch Mark got into it too. Ms. Alcott asked Mark to pick up everyone's homework. He just walked by me. Left mine on my desk. So I said, 'Hey, Marky,' I didn't mean anything by it. I've always called him 'Marky.' Everybody did until sixth grade. He was at the front of the room and he said in a really high voice, 'What do you want, Baby Bear?' Everybody started laughing and he said it again, 'Baby Bear.' Even Jasmine and Devi were laughing. I jumped up, ran at him and shoved him hard."

His grandmother leaned back and raised a hand to her mouth. "Oh, your mother didn't say—"

Bear had to rush and tell the hard part before he lost his nerve. "I guess Ms. Alcott was coming over. To tell him to stop. That's what she said. When I hit Mark it knocked him into her and they both fell down with Mark on top of Ms. Alcott in front of the whole class." Bear shook his head at the memory of the two of them on the floor and the whole class shocked into silence.

His grandmother sat with both hands in front of her mouth.

"Mom didn't tell you?"

"She said you had 'a small altercation' at school." His grandmother folded her napkin. "It was hard for her to talk about. Or she didn't want me to know. I don't know."

"I'm suspended for a week." Bear's voice was so quiet he could barely hear himself. "For assaulting a student and a teacher." Bear twisted his napkin while he waited for his grandmother's lecture to start. When he heard only silence he glanced at her. She was staring down and chewing on her lower lip.

"Bear, I will always love you. You know that." She pushed her chair back and said, "But I am disappointed that you lost your temper. I can't pretend not to be." She picked up his dinner plate. "Not hungry tonight?" and bustled into the kitchen.

She was disappointed. He knew she would be. There was nothing he could say that would make either of them feel better about what he had done. Without saying "good night," being told to brush his teeth, or even a bedtime hug, he snuck upstairs followed by Honey the Wonder Dog. Bear pulled the door shut behind them, left the light off and lay down on top of the quilt his grandmother had made for him when he was born. Honey plopped on the floor beside him and instantly fell asleep. Bear reached down to rub one of her silky ears and watched her paws quiver. She was chasing something in her dreams. The weight of Bear's sadness pinned him to the bed. He had disappointed his grandmother and he did not know how to say he was sorry.

3

In the morning, Bear opened his eyes and saw Honey's snout inches from his face. She stared eagerly back at him. As soon as he reached out to scratch her head, her tail began swishing across the wooden floor. The year Bear was born the neighbors had started calling her Honey the Wonder Dog.

One morning, when Honey was a year old, his grandmother had gotten up, let the dog out, and then started the coffee and made breakfast. Fifteen minutes later, when she opened the door to let Honey back into the house, Honey had the *Portland Press Herald*, neatly rolled up with a rubber band around it, in her mouth. Sally Parker made a quick guess that the paper had been delivered to the Professor's house. She dashed across the dirt road and placed it quietly on his front porch. That evening, when she was working in her garden, the Professor strolled over and mentioned that Gus, the newspaper delivery man, had accidentally left a paper at his house that morning. Bear's grandmother pretended not to know anything about the misplaced newspaper.

The following morning Honey returned with another newspaper in her mouth and her tail wagging. Bear's grandmother knew she couldn't simply leave the paper on another neighbor's porch and hope she was right. Instead she poured a cup of coffee, pulled a chair over to the window with the widest view of Maple Street and waited for Gus to return. If someone were missing their paper they would call Gus. He would gladly return. The only reason he had the job was because of his lifelong habit of getting up early. Retirement had not changed his sleep patterns. He enjoyed the morning drive around the island greeting and checking in on his neighbors. Always clad in a button-down shirt and khaki pants, he was a well-dressed paperboy. "No sense in leaving perfectly good clothes hanging in the closet," he'd say. As Sally Parker waited, she read the paper and did the crossword puzzle. After an hour, Gus parked in front of Viola Frost's home. Bear's grandmother dropped the paper on the floor, ran out to meet Gus and signed up for a newspaper subscription. She hadn't planned on that but decided she enjoyed the morning routine, and this way Honey could continue bringing her the paper without stealing from the neighbors.

Sally had carried Mrs. Frost's paper to the elderly woman who sat waiting patiently on her front porch. She chuckled as her neighbor alternated between explaining and apologizing for Honey's behavior.

"No need to apologize. She didn't steal my paper. She paid for it."

"What?"

"Well, I didn't know that at the time, but she left me two lovely apples, placed them right there," Mrs. Frost gestured toward the welcome mat, "where the paper should have been. Of course, they were a bit soggy. But there wasn't a tooth mark in any of them or I might have guessed. In all my life I've never seen a dog quite like her. She's a wonder." And she had been Honey the Wonder Dog ever since.

After a few days, Gus and Honey the Wonder Dog had worked out a routine. When she heard his car turn onto Maple Street she ran to the edge of the road and sat. Gus would drive up, give her a treat, and hand her the newspaper. For eleven years she had been faithfully delivering Sally Parker's newspaper.

Bear smelled his grandmother's coffee as he lay in bed, still dressed in the clothes he'd worn to school the day before. There was a blanket covering him. His grandmother must have tucked him in after he had fallen asleep. He was reluctant to go downstairs, anxious about how she would greet him after last night's discussion. His stomach

rumbled. He knew she had fresh Maine blueberries waiting for him. But even that was not enough to pull him from
his bedroom.

"Hey, Honey, let's see what Mom packed. Maybe there's
a treat in there for you."

Honey the Wonder Dog licked his face before moving
to sit next to the suitcase, staring intently at the black bag
as her tail thumped against the bed.

Bear knelt beside her, unzipping slowly, remembering
how heavy it had been. As heavy as a backpack with every
book a sixth grader could use in a full school day, he thought.
But when he lifted the lid he was surprised to see his binoculars and a stack of his favorite Marvel comic books. He
grinned at Honey but she continued to stare and lowered
her nose down between the stacks of neatly folded clothes.

"You smell something don't you?" Bear shuffled through
the carefully organized layers. Sure enough, his mother
had thrown in one of Honey's favorite chew treats. The dog
popped up eagerly as Bear handed it to her. She circled twice
before laying down with the treat between her front paws.

When he removed the comic books he saw a manila
envelope with his full name, Berend Houtman, written
neatly in cursive. It had to be from Ms. Alcott. Bear sat on
the floor and propped his back against the bed, prepared
for the worst. Honey paused in her chewing to tilt her head
and look concerned.

Dear Berend,

I know that the choices you made today do not reflect who you truly are. I understand from some of your classmates that you have been bullied since the first day of school. I want to apologize to you for failing to see this and halt the teasing. That is my responsibility as your teacher and I let you down. I am truly sorry.

Your responsibility as a student is to ask for help when you need it, whether it's a problem with math or a bully. I understand why you were upset today. I'm sure I would have been too <u>but</u> that does not excuse your shoving Mark. I'm sure you understand that someone could have been seriously hurt. Also, it's important that you learn that people have the right to be called by a name of their choosing. It is disrespectful to call you Baby Bear and to call him Marky if you two have outgrown those names.

For the next week you will be a student on Oxbow Island. This is not a suspension but an alternate placement. Your parents, the principal, and I all agree that you don't need to be punished. You need time to develop a successful strategy for sixth grade. During this week your grandmother will be in charge of your education.

Sincerely,

Ms. Alcott

Bear stopped reading and jumped up. "Gramma!" He ran down the stairs with the letter in his hand and Honey close behind him. "Gramma, you didn't tell me…"

The Professor was sitting across from her holding a cup of coffee and suggesting words for the crossword puzzle his grandmother was working on. Bear stopped and Honey crashed into the back of his legs.

"Good morning, Mr. Bear," the Professor said with his usual formality.

"Good morning, Professor." Bear looked at his grandmother.

She raised her eyebrows and gave him a faint smile before returning to her crossword puzzle. She didn't seem mad, sad, or disappointed. That was good but she should have told him that she was going to be his teacher.

"You can call me 'Mr. Yeats,'" the Professor said.

"What? Why?" Bear plopped onto the couch next to his grandmother, staring at the Professor. Honey groaned as she lowered herself onto Bear's feet.

"Because that's my surname."

Bear looked at his grandmother. Her smile was wide but she ignored him and pretended to be focused on her crossword puzzle. He looked back at the Professor.

"Sally, your grandmother, has employed me to be your instructor for the next week. I could demand that you call me Professor Yeats as my other pupils do but that seems excessive. Now, when I say she hired me, I mean that we are bartering for your academic instruction. You will be stacking my firewood in exchange for tutorial services."

How could bad news turn into good news and then back to bad news so quickly? Bear wondered. Is this what growing up was all about? You never get to relax and just enjoy the things you've looked forward to? Bear balanced his teacher's letter on Honey's head and looked back at the Professor. "But why Yeats?"

"It's the name that was bestowed upon me by my parents."

"You never knew his name? I just call him the Professor. It's a nickname."

Bear and Honey looked back and forth between the two adults.

"Your grandmother has been referring to me as the Professor since I was approximately your age." He smiled. "I always had my face stuck in a book. Truth be told, she used to call me 'The Little Professor.'"

"Little?" Bear asked skeptically of the tallest person he knew.

"There was a time when I was your size. Did you think I was born this tall?" The Professor did not wait for an answer. "My name is Malcolm Yeats. I have the names of an American civil rights activist and an Irish poet." He tapped his heart with pride and then looked at Sally Parker.

"It appears that even the people we have known for a lifetime can surprise us."

"Sorry, I didn't know your real name. Guess it never came up." Bear looked at his shoes as he spoke. "Does your nickname, the Professor, bother you?"

"No," he answered without hesitation. "I am a professor now. I've often wondered if your grandmother's nickname motivated me to work hard in school and pursue my education. I grew into my name."

Bear tried to imagine having an inspirational nickname: Panda Bear, Koala Bear, Bare End…it was hopeless.

His grandmother set her pencil down and said, "Your Auntie A, when she was four, was asked if she preferred to be called Alexandra or Alex, and she said, 'I prefer to be called Cinderella.'"

Bear started laughing. "Really? Auntie A?" He couldn't imagine anyone calling his lawyer aunt "Cinderella."

"My point is, some names stick because they fit. Others just fade away." His grandmother nodded her head and ruffled his curly hair. "It's good to see you smiling again. Are you happy to be here?"

"Yes, but…" his voice faded and he paused. "How's this school thing going to work?" he asked his grandmother before turning to Malcolm Yeats. "How much wood?" Before he could answer, Bear continued, "And what do you know about sixth grade? You're a college professor." Then he saw the letter still resting on Honey's head and held it up for them to see. "Did you know I'm not suspended? She says it's a—" Bear looked down at the letter—"an 'alternate placement,' that's what she said. And Ms. Alcott apologized to me. Can you believe that?" Bear looked back and forth at his grandmother and Mr. Yeats, who were quietly studying him.

The Professor broke the silence. "It's becoming apparent that I have rather large shoes to fill."

"What? Professor, sometimes you don't make any sense!"

"It's Mr. Yeats to you, young man, and it's an expression signifying that Ms. Alcott is an excellent teacher. Let's discuss your academic schedule."

Bear groaned. "But it's Saturday."

"Bear, don't interrupt your teacher." His grandmother sounded like she was enjoying this.

"First things first. Your grandmother has prepared a nutritious breakfast for you. After you eat that you need to report to your first class."

Bear slouched down on the couch with his arms across his chest and glared at Mr. Yeats.

The Professor continued. "You are to take Honey the Wonder Dog into the woods and complete preliminary research on the trails. I expect to see a draft by lunchtime. This will include a rough sketch of the trails, assessment of their condition, need for clearing, and location of resources: berries, ponds, and other points of interest."

Bear sat up. "You want me to spend the morning in the woods, with Honey and a sketch pad?"

"Precisely."

Bear could barely contain his excitement as he and Honey jumped up and ran toward the kitchen. Halfway to the table it occurred to him that if he looked too eager they might make the first assignment harder. He slowed down and hung his head just in case they were watching.

"Remember, it's due at lunchtime." The door slammed shut behind the Professor.

4

Bear ate his breakfast in gulps before racing to the door with Honey close behind him.

"Whoa, Buckaroo, aren't you forgetting something?" his grandmother asked as she stepped between him and the door.

"Right!" Bear turned and ran upstairs. He grabbed his backpack, binoculars, sketch pad, and a pencil before loudly clomping back down the stairs to where Honey sat waiting patiently.

"I packed you some snacks," his grandmother said as she handed him a paper bag and a water bottle. "And some bags, in case you see any blackberries. Plus, I need more rose hips for tea."

"Got it!" Bear said as he shoved the bags into his backpack before reaching for the door knob one more time.

"Honey's leash," she prompted. "Now keep that on her. Gus said they hired an animal control officer and he's looking for off-leash dogs."

Bear clipped it onto Honey's collar and headed out the door. He took the porch steps two at a time and ran down the dirt road, eager to get to the woods. As soon as he was out of sight of his grandmother's house, he stopped and held the palm of his hand in front of Honey's face, signaling her to sit. Her tail swept back and forth as Bear carefully folded the leash before handing it to Honey, who gently clasped it in her mouth. The leash was still attached, but now she was walking herself.

"Don't tell Gramma," Bear whispered and winked. Honey winked back. "You're the best friend ever," he said, scratching behind her ears. "Let's go!" With that command, the boy and dog trotted side by side to the end of the road and the start of the trail. It was a well-worn path weaving through tall trees and low fragrant ferns, visible to those who knew to look for it.

They sped up and didn't stop until they were standing on a mossy ridge beside a pine tree that had blown down in the last storm. The road was out of sight. The woods enveloped them. Bear took a deep breath; the scent of pine needles, musty decaying logs, and salty ocean air filled him. As soon as he unclipped Honey's leash and took it from her, she raced over to the small brook and waded in for a drink beside the rough log bridge.

Taking off his backpack, Bear heard a soft tapping high above him. With a quiet slap of his hand against his thigh, he called Honey back to him and gave her the pointer signal. Her nose instantly shot up in the direction of the tapping. After a moment she lifted one leg and aimed her paw at the woodpecker. Bear looked through his binoculars at the branch indicated by Honey's pointing. As he focused the lenses he saw he was right. The tapping was too quiet to come from a crow-sized pileated woodpecker. It was a downy woodpecker, about the size of his hand and not nearly as shy as the larger birds. The black-and-white wings reminded him of a checkered flag. The red patch on the back of its head let Bear know he was watching a male boring into the tree branch, eating insects. A long line of holes drilled deep into the pine tree's trunk indicated there were other woodpeckers in the area. In his sketch book he began his trail map with a mark for the Woodpecker Tree.

Two trails looped around the wooded interior of the northern and southern halves of Oxbow Island. Many smaller trails crisscrossed through the woods within those loops. Bear decided to start with the North Loop Trail. This would eventually bring him back to the woodpecker tree. Years earlier, someone had removed the tops and bottoms from tin cans and nailed them to the trees along the trail.

Several steps past each marker, you could look ahead and see the next one guiding you forward. When the angle of the sun was just right, the metal flashed and sparkled, making them easier to locate.

They would walk the roughest part first. His grandmother had said it was nearly impassable since the Patriot's Day Storm. Six months earlier, something like a miniature tornado had hit that part of the island and knocked down so many trees that the trail had almost disappeared. Bear was eager for an adventure.

The North Loop Trail began with the Long Log Bridge. Crossing it required balance and focus. Years back, a tall pine tree had fallen across the widest spot in the brook. Someone had sawed off the top six inches, creating a narrow, flat balance beam for hikers. Bear paused to draw this on his map while Honey raced across the skinny bridge. Bear put his arms out to his sides for balance and slowly walked the twenty feet across the large tree trunk. When he got to Honey, he saw that she was already muddy from paws to belly.

As they continued into the woods, Bear paid close attention to the woodland noises. High above them two tree limbs made an eerie screeching as they rubbed against each other in the breeze. He smiled. When Bear was younger, that sound had convinced him the woods were haunted. He had refused to go walking with his grandmother until she had persuaded him that Honey the Wonder Dog would keep them safe.

Bear heard twigs snapping in the woods to his left. He dropped to his knees and raised his right hand to stop Honey. Bear edged behind a large mossy rock and Honey followed his example. They sat in silence, staring toward a narrow overgrown path that often had deer tracks on it. With binoculars raised, he listened closely and heard the sound of rustling leaves before aiming the binoculars in that direction, hoping to see at least one deer nibbling at the underbrush.

As he focused the binoculars, he wasn't sure what he was seeing but he knew it wasn't a deer. Bear lowered the binoculars and saw a flash of red before peering through the binoculars again. There was a person—the back of a person—with short black hair, mud-covered knee-high rain boots, and a green-and-gray shirt that faded into the foliage. On the stranger's back was a large basket, nearly half the size of the person. Around its upper edge was a red stripe. It was impossible to tell if he was looking at a man or a woman. Bear watched in silence as the person moved quietly away from him, occasionally kneeling and then silently throwing something into the basket.

When the stranger had been out of sight for several minutes, Bear slowly rose to his feet. "That was weird," he whispered to Honey. "Who's that? What's that person doing?" Bear considered the possibilities. The dog was not interested in his questions. She was already trotting down the trail toward the beaver pond. Bear rushed to catch up with her.

They scrambled up a steep rocky incline. At the top they could see all the damage the Patriot's Day Storm had done. Giant trees lay on their sides. Branches reached for the sky as the trunks had before the winds. The shallow roots were now as tall as they had once been wide, rising high above his head. There were boulders entangled in them as if they had grasped onto the stones in a final desperate attempt to remain buried below the layer of topsoil.

The island, only five miles in circumference, was essentially a giant rock bursting from the ocean floor. Someone had told him that, over millions of years, a thin fertile layer of topsoil had been created from decay and nature's litter of leaves, pine needles, and rotting plants. In this area it was only a foot or two deep. When strong winds blew, the fifty-foot-tall pitch pine and white pine trees swayed back and forth. If one fell it could knock over three or more on its way down, eliminating the wind block for the next line of trees. On this side of the hill every tree lay on the ground. It looked like a giant had stopped by to play a game of pickup sticks.

The path was covered and it was hard to tell which way to go with all the familiar markers thrown aside. They paused as Bear tried to remember where to turn. Honey set out at a steady pace, trotting under the first tree, which was propped up several feet in the air by the branches that had been driven into the ground. Bear followed Honey, crawling on his hands and knees. At the next downed tree, Honey went under, squeezing between two branches, while Bear scrambled over rather than risk being pinned beneath the giant tree. Facing the sky was the bottom of a tin can nailed to the trunk, sparkling in the sun, marking a trail that had vanished. Tree by tree they scrambled, often forced to backtrack when they couldn't find a passageway between branches, over and under trunks, across the rocky, steep terrain.

At the bottom of the hill they had to cross the brook again. The water was shallow but the brook's muddy path was too wide to jump over. Bear took several steps in each direction, looking for a place to cross. Honey jumped up on the tree trunk that had fallen across the brook and carefully zigzagged around branches, avoiding the muck below. Bear followed her lead and held on to the branches for balance.

Safely on the other side, proud of their efforts navigating the tree-strewn obstacle course, he made some notes on his map. He wondered if it would be possible to return and limb up this tree to create another log bridge like the one at the beginning of the trail. When he looked up from his sketch pad he saw Honey, her golden fur glowing in the sunshine as she rolled enthusiastically on some dead animal or scat that was guaranteed to stink.

"Honey! No! Stop!" Bear hollered as he rushed toward the golden retriever.

At the sound of the boy's voice, Honey popped up and wagged her tail. It was hard to stay mad at a dog.

Back on the trail they sped up, practically running, eager to get to the beaver pond. This pond had been dug over a hundred years earlier, before people had refrigerators. In the winters when it froze, the islanders had cut giant blocks of ice and shipped them to Boston, New York, and Philadelphia. In the past decade, beavers had taken over. With two new dams slowing the flow of water out of the pond, it had grown as a result and was now surrounded by wetlands that attracted migrating birds. The pond was dotted with dome-like beaver lodges made from branches and twigs held together by mud.

With the pond in sight, Bear and Honey slowed and moved quietly, hoping to catch a glimpse of a beaver. There was plenty of evidence that the beavers had been busy: trees with deep indentations circling their trunks a foot or two above the ground; other trees that had been chewed through and fallen over before the beavers gnawed all the bark off the trunk. Smaller branches had been dragged to the pond and used to build dams and lodges where the beavers would live through the frozen months. As Bear and Honey crept to the edge of the pond they were startled by a loud splash. Bear saw the ripples on the surface of the water in the middle of the pond, where the beaver had dived after slapping his tail to warn the rest of his family.

The beaver's alarm was also heard by a great blue heron fishing at the pond's edge. The large bird slowly flew to a hidden spot on the far side of the water. Bear waited patiently for the beaver to resurface. Eventually, he was able to spot the outline of the beaver's flat head, with eyes, nose, and ears barely above the water's surface, gliding silently across the water toward the opposite edge of the pond.

Bear rested his back against a stump with a jagged point and ate the oatmeal raisin cookies his grandmother had packed for him. There was even a treat for Honey. While he made notes in his sketchbook, Honey dozed with her head across his outstretched legs. With the sun warming them and the quiet of the woods, all the embarrassment and hurt of Bear's first week of sixth grade evaporated.

Before heading to the birch grove, he needed to check the small cranberry bog his family relied on at Thanksgiving. Bear made his way around the edge of the pond, past the upright long-stemmed leaves of several jack-in-the-pulpits with clusters of shiny red berries. The water was high and he wondered if there would be any cranberries for their Thanksgiving supper. When he saw footprints sunken into the dark slushy mud at the edge of the pond, he paused. They marked the way to the cranberry bog. The footprints were so deep and clear they had to be fresh. Was it possible that the person with the basket had been here too? Maybe he and his grandmother weren't the only ones who relied on this spot for their annual cranberry relish. Bear moved forward slowly, and was relieved to see that the cranberries appeared untouched. He would have to return and check them again in a few days.

Heading toward the cluster of birch trees, Bear began wondering about the mysterious basket person. It had to be the same person who'd left the footprints at the cranberry bog. In all the years he had been coming here with his grandmother they had never encountered anyone this far from the major trails. Whoever the mystery person was, he or she seemed to know these woods.

The white birch bark glistened in the bright sunshine as the leaves flickered in the breeze. Bear had always considered this the most peaceful place on earth. He turned slowly, staring up at the blue sky through the shifting branches. Beneath the quiet he could hear the air moving through the trees. Honey nudged his knee with her nose, interrupting his reverie. She sat and pointed. The bright red flash of a male cardinal darted past them. There is magic in these trees, Bear thought.

Just beyond the lowland birch the ground rose up a bit and there was less sunlight as the dense pine woods replaced the lacy birch trees. That's where he would find the pink lady's slippers, a tiny orchid and his favorite flower.

They wouldn't be flowering now, but Bear could easily spot the plants' two broad oval leaves. He and his grandmother had been checking on these plants for years, and had even seen a few with white flowers, in spite of their name. The mapping assignment the Professor had given him could be used to track the lady's slippers. The tender orchids grew in small clusters that seemed to be getting a little larger with each passing year. This week he would mark down each location and begin to keep a more accurate count of the plants' progress.

When Bear had first discovered the delicate pink flowers, just one per plant, dangling from the end of each stem, he had wanted to gather a bouquet for his mother. His grandmother told him the legend of an Ojibwe girl who had run for miles and miles barefoot through the snow to get medicine for her tribe. After returning with the medicine, she had collapsed with red, frozen, swollen feet. The fragile flowers appeared at the spots her feet had touched to mark her heroic efforts to save her tribe. His grandmother also explained it was wrong to dig them up or pick them. They wouldn't survive transplanting and cutting the flowers meant they wouldn't spread or appear the next year.

Bear spotted the bench made from a fallen tree. He walked past that and slowed, remembering where several plants had been that summer. He scanned the earth for the oval green leaves. Bear was sure he was in the right spot as he looked off the trail to the base of a pine tree and a rotting fallen log. They should be right here. He paused to add the log bench to his sketch before staring at the packed dirt in front of his feet. They should be there, but he didn't see them. When he stepped off the trail he noticed a circle of bare soil inside a ring of pine needles, twigs, and leaves. Someone had pulled back a layer of woods debris. Inside the cleared circle were five bowl-sized divots dug in the soft soil. He dropped to his knees and rubbed his hand across the bottom of each hole. Honey noticed Bear's distress and sat beside him, sticking her nose into each cavity.

"Someone stole the lady's slippers!" His eyes were wide with concern. "We have to get back and tell Gramma." He shoved the notebook and binoculars back in his backpack. The mapping assignment would have to wait. Now he needed to get back to his grandmother's the fastest way possible, and that meant taking a narrow deer path out of the woods.

They ran toward Club Road, emerging from the trees opposite the Yacht Club. Sailboat masts bobbed gently in the marina. The asphalt felt hard as their feet struck the firm surface. Bear was out of breath, but he had to get back to his grandmother's house. She would know what to do. The sound of his feet slapping against the road was no longer matched by Honey's claws as Bear approached the Tennis Club. He looked down. She wasn't there. He stopped and turned back to see her sitting in the road next to a large clump of wild rugosa roses.

"Come on," he hollered, but she wouldn't budge. Frustrated, Bear walked back to her, repeating, "Come on, Honey." She sat with her nose in the air. Was she pointing at a rare bird for him? "We gotta go," he said to the stubborn dog. Suddenly, Bear understood. "The rose hips? Gramma's rose hips?"

Bear dropped his backpack on the road, fished out one of the plastic bags his grandmother had given him, and started picking the rose's fruit: orange-red and the size of gumballs, they were the opposite of candy: sour, healthy, and packed with vitamins. Not at all like a gumball. Bear tried to avoid being scratched by thorns as he reached into the bush for rose hips that hadn't been pecked by birds. When his bag was full, he turned to Honey and said, "Now can we go?"

She jumped up and wagged her tail, letting him know she was satisfied. Bear ran the rest of the way, cradling his backpack and the rose hips against his chest. He started hollering when he was in the middle of the road in front of her house. "Gramma! Gramma!"

"What?" She was on the porch before her grandson's foot hit the first step.

Bear bent over to catch his breath.

"Where's Honey's leash?" his grandmother asked disapprovingly.

Bear waved away her question. "Someone stole the lady's slippers!"

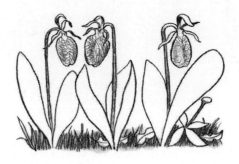

5

"What seems to be the problem?" the Professor asked. He strolled across the street in response to Bear's yelling. "It's awfully early. Have you completed your assignment?"

"No, no, I—" Bear began

"Berend, is everything all right?" Mrs. Frost hollered. She had stuck her head out an open window on the first floor of her house. The window was next to the card table where she spent her days on jigsaw puzzles, "correspondence," and "watching the world go by." Not that a great deal of the world passed down their dirt road even during the busiest summer days on Oxbow Island. "I heard the ruckus."

"The lady's slippers. In the woods. Someone stole the lady's slippers! I think I saw them," Bear said. His frustration with the adults around him was obvious.

The announcement was greeted with a stunned silence followed by murmuring:

"Oh, dear."

"That should be a federal offense."

"They'll never survive being transplanted."

"What're we going to do? We have to do something. We can't just stand here," Bear was practically yelling as his eyes darted from adult to adult, waiting for a plan.

Mrs. Frost surprised Bear by being the first to speak, and she did it with an urgency he had never heard from his grandmother's elderly neighbor. "Berend's right. Sally, call the taxi. Berend, give the Professor a clear description of the suspect. We've got work to do." Then her head popped back inside the window and it slammed shut.

"Well, I don't know if it's a man or a woman, but the thief has a big backpack basket, short black hair, and really muddy boots. "And is about Gramma's height."

Bear bounded down the porch stairs and raced next door with the Professor right behind him, eager to learn what Mrs. Frost had planned. He could hear her before he saw her hobbling wobbly frame.

As soon as her front door opened, she was explaining to the Professor and Bear: "I don't believe he could have made the 10 o'clock boat with those plants. Those orchids are very fragile and will need to be transplanted as soon as possible."

Bear's grandmother appeared on the porch. "The taxi's on its way. What are we doing?"

Mrs. Frost, with the Professor at her elbow said, "By my calculations they'll try to make their escape on the 11 o'clock. Zoe should be here." At that moment they heard the taxi turn onto Maple Street, and all heads swiveled to see the plume of dust stirred up by the speeding driver. The island taxi was a dented cherry-red minivan with a suitcase tied to the roof. The brakes squealed, announcing its arrival, and Mrs. Frost smiled. "There she is." A young woman jumped out of the van and sprinted to Mrs. Frost. Her dark brown dreadlocks bounced against her back and her long flowery skirt blew up to reveal a pair of jeans and hiking boots.

"Who's the tree-hugging hippie?" Bear whispered to his grandmother.

"Be nice." His grandmother gave him a stern look. "Her name's Zoe and she's a lovely person."

"Malcolm, ride with Zoe. Share the details: crime and the suspect's description. You two will search the departing crowd." As Mrs. Frost turned to face Bear and his grandmother, the taxi doors slammed shut before departing with a screech and a new plume of exhaust. "You two will alert the police."

At the sound of their orders, Bear and his grandmother trotted down the road.

Traffic on Oxbow Island was predictable: ten minutes before and after the ferry docked there was a flood of walkers, cyclists, cars, and trucks rushing to and from Wharf Street. People double parked, made illegal U-turns, or ran down the middle of the street pushing shopping carts and spilling coffee with every step. The intersection of Water and Wharf Streets was more likely to resemble a demolition derby than a sleepy island crossroads for the next twenty minutes. Once the boat left, the island quickly absorbed the hundreds who came over to ride their bikes, walk, or visit friends, along with those who were returning home after a trip to Portland for groceries or a doctor's appointment.

The island police officer always parked near the ferry dock. The police met every boat. Why was a mystery. Some joked that the boat's schedule was a criminal's guide for when to commit crimes on the back side of the island. With each boat the officer on duty would sit serenely in the police cruiser. Meanwhile, drivers waiting for the ferry often argued about someone cutting in the long line of cars as large groups of tourists and day-trippers stood in the middle of the road blocking all traffic while they chatted about the sights on Oxbow Island. As tempers flared and horns honked, the officer invariably sat in the police car ignoring the chaos. The police did not consider these conflicts and disruptions to be crimes. But they were major offenses to the residents of Oxbow Island.

Bear and his grandmother knew they would find the police car backed in at the top of the dock. Out of breath, they reached the intersection of Water and Wharf Street and saw the taxi stuck behind a blob of ice-cream eating tourists posing for pictures in the middle of the road. On the other side of the crowd, driving up the hill was the first car disembarking the ferry. The taxi's horn bleated, startling the vacationers.

The Professor jumped out of the taxi. His height commanded attention. His thick glasses reflected the sunlight, bright against his dark skin as his head swiveled above the throng growing around him. His voice boomed. "Esteemed travelers, if you would be kind enough to step aside." With his arms spread wide, he herded the distracted camera-toting multitudes out of the taxi's path and into the path of the cars disembarking the ferry.

In the crowd, the residents of Oxbow Island all turned their attention from the taxi to Erin the deckhand. Nobody got in the way of Erin when she was in charge of loading and unloading the ferry. This could be amusing or terrifying, but it would end up being a great story told and retold either way.

Erin took two large strides up the hill, her face as red as a stop sign. "No! No! No!" Her arms waved in front of her. They swung above her head. She crossed them like an

X. She flapped them vigorously to the side. She hollered "Noooo!" Her voice was unrecognizable.

"Erin." The Professor waved his arms high above the crowd to get her attention and yelled, "Brief moment of disruption. Nothing more. It's an emergency."

She spun toward his voice. She glared at her watch. She glared at the Professor. And then Erin crossed her arms and glared at the taxi. It seemed that the whole island froze and held its breath, waiting.

Zoe tooted the taxi's horn, drove over the curb, veered left and then right around clumps of day-trippers who didn't have the sense to get out of the way. Eventually she disappeared into the parking lot.

Once the taxi was out of sight, Erin turned her impatience on the drivers waiting to drive off the ferry. She waved the first driver forward with a jerk of her hand that suggested he had been responsible for the delay.

Bear had not seen anything "lovely" about Zoe, but her driving was impressive. His grandmother knocked on the window of the police car. Officer Calvin was still staring in the direction of the taxi's swerving route into the parking lot. He was startled by the sight of the boy and his grandmother peering through the window at him.

When the officer lowered the window, Bear blurted, "We're here to report a robbery!"

"Get in." Officer Calvin grinned. "We're going to the station," he said without hesitation.

Bear jumped into the front seat. His grandmother hopped in the back. The police officer switched on his lights and siren and the road suddenly cleared in front of them. Once again, Erin thrust her arms in front of her as her face darkened; she was forced to halt the disembarking cars again. She glared at them with a gaze that made Bear quiver, but Officer Calvin was oblivious to the deckhand's fury. As the police car sped up the hill, Bear continued to look back at Erin, expecting her hair to burst into flames or her head to explode.

Officer Calvin spoke into his hand-held radio, "Two, one, one on Oxbow Island." He sounded eager and was beaming at them. He must be happy to finally have a real crime to investigate, Bear thought, feeling proud that he was responsible for the officer's sudden enthusiasm.

The attentive smile remained stuck on Officer Calvin's face when they were seated in the one-room police station. With an official police report form on the table between them, he gripped his pen and leaned forward. "Start at the beginning." He looked directly at Bear's grandmother as he spoke. "Tell me exactly what happened. Be as detailed as possible."

She glanced at Bear and gave him a nudge. The eleven-year-old slid to the front of his creaky plastic chair, nervously swinging his feet, and cleared his throat. "Well, I was in the woods this morning with Honey the Wonder Dog. She's my grandmother's dog. We were mapping the trails for…" he paused to consider exactly how much detail the officer wanted, "…for a school assignment. On the North Loop Trail, before it divides, there's a deer trail. We saw a person there. I can't tell you if it was a man or a woman, even though I looked really close with my binoculars. But I did see short black hair, muddy, muddy, really muddy boots, and a big basket on the person's back. They're about as tall as my grandmother, I think."

Bear noticed that the officer's smile was fading and he hadn't written one word on his police form. "Oh, and they were wearing a plaid shirt, almost like camo, green and gray, but it was plaid. It blended in with the trees really well."

Bear looked at the skeptical officer. "Gramma's neighbors are down at the boat right now looking for him. Or her. It could have been a her," he said in an attempt to reassure the police officer.

"Son," the policeman's voice dropped an octave as he leaned toward Bear, "*what* was stolen?"

Startled by the officer's change in attitude, Bear blurted, "Pink lady's slippers."

"Shoes." Officer Calvin shook his head and wrote something on his form then looked at Sally Parker. "Your shoes?"

"No, no, no." She shook her head.

"It's a plant. A kind of orchid."

Officer Calvin set down his pen and pushed the official form toward the middle of the gray table before looking back at Sally Parker. "Someone stole some plants from your garden?"

"No!" Bear immediately realized he had yelled at an officer of the law. He gulped some air attempting to calm himself, but it sounded like a burp. "They're practically endangered," his voice cracked. Blushing, he attempted to push through his embarrassment. "It should be a federal offense to dig them up. They're very fragile. You should never, ever, try to transplant them. That's why we're here." His voice had nearly sunk to a whisper, but he had to make Officer Calvin understand. He gripped the seat of his chair. "My grandmother would never have lady's slippers in her garden. Someone dug them up in the woods. He stole them."

"So, those missing slippers don't belong to either one of you," Officer Calvin said before standing up and pushing in his chair.

Bear and his grandmother spoke to his uniformed back as he rearranged piles of paperwork on the counter. They tried to explain the urgency of the crime, but no matter what they said, Officer Calvin had made up his mind. He silently put his pen in the desk drawer. He straightened the pile of blank police report forms, and then walked to the door and held it open. His attitude was obvious. He saw this as another typical day on Oxbow Island, where the hysterical residents viewed a lost bike as a crime wave. Another event that would lead islanders to complain, "The police never do anything," and the police would respond, "That's because there's nothing to do."

Bear and his grandmother left the police station feeling dejected, and immediately saw the Professor. He was smiling from ear to ear.

"Why're you here?" Bear asked. "Did you catch him?"

"No, unfortunately there were no sightings of the alleged plant thief."

"What time is it? You should be waiting for the next ferry. They'll leave on that one for sure."

"No cause for alarm. Erin has offered to be on the lookout for your perpetrator. Everyone has to pass by her when they board the boat. It seemed like a logical solution."

"Erin? Erin the deckhand is helping us?" Bear was shocked. Officer Calvin had practically thrown them out of the police station but Erin, the crabby deckhand who seemed to enjoy yelling at small children, had offered to help.

"When I explained the potential impact of the environmental crime, she was eager to offer her assistance." The Professor looked at Bear's suspicious face before continuing. "You know she's a stickler for the rules. Simply cannot abide a scofflaw."

Bear had no idea what a scofflaw was, but he did know that Erin was always eager to catch a rule breaker.

With all sense of urgency and importance removed from their day, it was agreed that Bear would head to Mooney's Market to buy bread and lunch meats for a hearty lunch before spending the afternoon stacking wood and waiting to hear from Erin. In front of the store, two couples dressed in white and carrying tennis rackets were in an animated discussion, blocking the entrance. Bear tried to be patient and polite as he stood behind the evenly tanned and fit foursome.

"The destruction is catastrophic," said the woman wearing a white visor.

"What are we supposed to do?" the bald man asked.

Bear sighed loudly, hoping they would notice him and get out of his way.

A man with a curly-cue moustache and bushy eyebrows bounced a tennis ball on his racket. He grinned and said, "I say we shoot them and call it target practice."

Now they had Bear's attention. With his mouth hanging open, he looked up at the assembled adults.

The second woman swept back her blond hair and laid a hand on the mustachioed man's shoulder. "Don't be silly, dear. You know you can't shoot beavers."

"Beavers? You want to shoot beavers?" Bear shook his head and pushed his way through the adults without waiting for an answer. The mustachioed man dropped his tennis ball.

"What a rude little boy," the blond woman said.

Bear shuffled slowly through the small grocery store. Deep in thought about the odd events of the morning, *rude little boy* repeating endlessly in his head, he grabbed a loaf of bread without even checking to see who was working the cash register or what the daily specials were. He skipped the candy aisle and went straight to the deli counter, alternately fuming at Officer Calvin, disgusted by the tennis players, and wondering if Erin was friendlier than he had assumed. Confused and preoccupied, he didn't look up until he heard Wanda, the deli clerk. When Bear turned toward the lunch meats he was startled to see, less than a foot in front of him, the basket person. He gasped. He took two steps backward. He had to be absolutely, positively sure that this was the right person. It was a girl, not an adult, a little bit older than he was, twelve or maybe thirteen. She was casually gesturing toward the red hot dogs

Bear's mind raced as he took inventory of the girl in front of him: muddy boots, plaid shirt the color of the woods, short black hair, a naturally tan complexion and a really big basket on her back. It was made of tightly woven birch switches. The flash of red was a drawstring for the fabric that lined the basket. Bear stood on his tiptoes and tried to look into the basket, but it was tightly closed. There was no doubt that this was the person they were looking for. He had to stop her before she escaped the island with the lady's slippers.

Alive with the urgency of the moment, he jumped between the girl and the deli counter. "What's in the basket?" he asked, trying to sound like a tough cop.

The girl looked down at him and sneered, "None of your business, creep. Get out of my way." She took her hot dogs off the deli counter and turned to leave.

Bear grabbed her by the arm. "Show me what you have in the basket or you're not going anywhere."

"Listen, runt." She spoke with a low hiss. "Let go of me or I'll knock you on your butt."

Her piercing brown eyes flashed at him. He could feel the muscles in her arm tense. That's when he realized she was bigger and probably stronger than he was.

"Bear." Without turning he knew it was Mr. Mooney, the store's owner. His voice was smooth like a game show host. "Is that any way to treat a lady?" he asked as he placed a hand on Bear's arm. When Bear didn't immediately loosen his grip, Mr. Mooney took a sterner tone. "Let go of Olivia right now, young man."

Bear dropped his arm to his side and felt his face redden. "But Mr. Mooney, I saw her in the woods, with that basket, this morning."

"So what?" Olivia said as she rubbed her arm where Bear had been gripping her. "You're lucky I didn't deck you."

"Olivia!" Mr. Mooney scolded, but he was starting to smile, too. "You are lucky she didn't hit you. She's got a mean right cross."

Bear was bursting with frustration. "You don't understand. She stole the pink lady's slippers."

"What?" they said in unison. Mr. Mooney appeared confused, and Olivia looked madder than she had when Bear grabbed her arm.

She swung the basket off her back and onto the floor beside her. Bear and Mr. Mooney raised their hands and took a step back as if preparing for her right cross. But Olivia dropped to her knees and began to open the basket.

"I would never dig up a lady's slipper. Do you think I'm an idiot? They need protecting. And, you can't transplant them. What kind of person do you think I am?" She was shaking her head with annoyance as she pulled open the basket's liner.

Bear and Mr. Mooney leaned forward to see what she had.

"What are they?" Bear asked.

"Mushrooms for dinner." Olivia removed two from the basket and held them up. "This is chicken of the woods and that's a puffball." The first mushroom looked like a yellow-and-orange pancake, while the other resembled a dirty ping-pong ball.

The three stood in a silent circle while Bear stared at the ground, using one foot to kick the other.

Mr. Mooney broke the silence, "You owe Olivia an apology."

"I know." Bear looked at the two of them and realized they expected more from him. He took a breath and blurted, "I'm really sorry. I shouldn't have grabbed you. I was upset about the lady's slippers and didn't know..." He looked at the tall girl glaring at him as she returned the basket to her back. "I really am sorry." His voice trailed off.

Olivia turned to walk away without saying another word.

"The hot dogs are on the house," Mr. Mooney hollered after her before turning to Bear. "You really are lucky she didn't hit you," he said with a chuckle.

6

Bear dropped the groceries on the kitchen counter before hollering, "Gramma!"

"I'm right here." She poked her head in from the dining room.

"Can I take Honey for a walk before lunch?"

"Of course." His grandmother looked into his eyes as she brushed the hair off his forehead. "Is everything all right? I know you're upset about the police not taking you seriously, but you did the right thing."

"It's okay." Bear did his best to sound and look like that was true, but he needed to go someplace quiet to sort everything out. He wasn't ready to tell his grandmother about Olivia and that there were people who thought it was funny to shoot beavers.

Clearly not believing her grandson, she kissed his forehead and said, "I love you," before adding, "Leash. Remember Honey's leash." At the sound of her words, Honey appeared in the doorway with the leash in her mouth and her tail thumping against the doorway.

Bear and Honey jogged to the woods path. As soon as they reached the woodpecker tree, Honey sat and Bear unhooked her leash. His mood lightened as he breathed in the scent of pine, ferns, and the decaying logs. Honey led the way, loping down the North Loop Trail before turning onto an overgrown, unmarked deer path. Bear, following her waving golden tail, couldn't remember ever going this way before. Ahead of him he noticed a tree that beavers had nearly gnawed through. How long before that would fall? But where's the water? Edging through the ferns on the right he could see a narrow stream. With each step, Bear saw more evidence of beaver activity. Where was Honey leading him? They turned a corner and Bear saw a pond. On the far side were four huge summer homes. The backshore, Atlantic Avenue, must be on the other side of those properties. He'd looped the island on that road hundreds of times but never known there was a pond behind those massive cottages. As Bear marveled at discovering a hidden pond, he heard a sound that froze his heart.

Honey the Wonder Dog cried out. Was it a yip or a yelp? He couldn't say, but his feet stumbled over themselves racing toward the golden retriever.

"Honey! Honey! I'm coming! Where are you? I'm coming. I'm coming." Breathless, he found her five feet off the path on the hidden pond's edge with her right front paw in a trap. Bear fell to the ground and tugged on the metal that gripped her paw as Honey whimpered. He wasn't strong enough to pull them apart. He wiped tears from his face and looked at Honey. She was counting on him. He couldn't run for help and leave her alone in pain. Bear jumped up and looked around. If he yelled would anyone in the summer houses hear him? Could he wedge a stick in there and pry the trap open? That might hurt her paw more. Honey whimpered quietly and Bear focused on the metal gripping her paw. There were two levers coming out from each side. He got down on his knees and pushed with all his weight. They moved but not enough. When Bear stood up, Honey's paw twitched in pain.

Bear took a deep breath. "Honey," he said as calmly as he could, "you have to trust me." She stopped thrashing and left her paw in front of him. Bear carefully put one foot on each lever and the trap popped open.

Honey pulled her paw out and licked it protectively. Bear used a twig to snap the trap shut so it wouldn't close on either of them again. He squatted beside Honey and wrapped his arms around her neck. "Can you walk? I'll carry you if I have to but we have to get out of here."

Honey tilted her head and raised an ear as if questioning his ability to carry her.

"Yeah, you're probably right." Bear sat back and thought. "Can I see your paw?" Bear put out his hand and Honey laid her injured paw on it. "I don't see any blood or a cut. That's good. Can I see if it bends?" When she didn't pull her paw back, Bear gently flexed it until she yipped and recoiled. "Can we try walking?" Bear stood and took two steps towards home, watching to see if Honey would follow. The golden retriever slowly rose and began walking on three legs. The injured paw was raised protectively to her chest.

"The trap—I should take the trap." Bear ran back and picked it up. They walked home slowly, silently, with Honey following in Bear's tracks. When they returned to the road, Bear attached Honey's leash and ruffled the fur on her head. "We're almost there. When we get home, I'll give you the best treat ever. Promise."

In spite of the promise, Honey's tail drooped between her legs.

"What's wrong?" Sally Parker yelled as she ran from Mrs. Frost's front porch to meet Bear and her limping dog.

Bear held up the trap.

His grandmother was on her knees hugging her dog and saying over and over again, "Honey, Honey, Honey."

When Bear looked up he saw the Professor and Mrs. Frost approaching. Mrs. Frost had tears in her eyes as she stared at her friend and the injured pet. The Professor was focused on the trap in Bear's hand.

"How dark is the heart of a human who wantonly injures innocent animals?" he asked with a quiet rage.

"I don't know," Bear stammered before he realized it was a question without an answer. "I got it off. It didn't cut her."

His grandmother gently examined Honey's paw and seemed to relax when she saw there was no sign of a wound. "I think you're going to be all right." She stood and smiled as Honey's tail thumped against Bear's leg.

Mrs. Frost put her arm around her neighbor's waist. "I'd say that's a good sign."

As they walked toward the porch for lunch, Honey used her injured paw. There was a slight limp, but she was walking on four legs again.

"Sally, I believe your canine companion is being stoic in an attempt to ease your sorrow," the Professor said.

Bear made himself a sandwich while his grandmother and Mrs. Frost asked endless questions and the Professor examined the long spring trap.

"Trappers are required to label all traps with their name and address." The Professor turned the trap over in his hands but there was no identification. "This individual would be classified as a poacher, not a trapper."

"Where were you?" "Was the trap hidden?" "How did you get the trap off?" His grandmother and Mrs. Frost spoke over each other as they reached for the lunch meats and condiments to make sandwiches for themselves.

"Honey is fortunate you had the skill and intellect to rapidly dislodge this device." The Professor gestured toward the trap he had set on the porch. "Otherwise she might have lost circulation in her paw, hurt herself, or bit you."

The women gasped and looked up from their food.

"My grandfather used to trap." The Professor stared at the long spring trap and nudged it with his foot. "Until he caught a bald eagle. Traps are indiscriminate. They don't select their victims."

Bear's grandmother patted his arm as he stared at the Professor. His heart froze with the thought of a bald eagle struggling against a steel trap until it died.

"What were they trying to catch?" Mrs. Frost said, more to herself than her neighbors. "That's the question. If we can answer it, we'll find the culprit."

"Let's assume they weren't trying to catch a golden retriever," the Professor began.

"Or a boy," his grandmother said as she gripped Bear's arm.

It hadn't occurred to Bear that he could have stepped in the trap.

"Or a bald eagle." The Professor's head drooped.

"Let's rule out children, household pets, and birds," Mrs. Frost began. "Either they were trapping for fur, like your grandfather, or trying to eliminate an animal they thought was a pest. Do you know what's in season now?"

The Professor shook his head.

"It's against the law to hunt on the island." His grand-mother was indignant. "Common sense says it's also against the law to trap."

"Common sense, it isn't very common anymore." Mrs. Frost nodded knowingly. "We can answer all these ques-tions with a quick call to the state after we finish our lunch." She picked some crumbs off her powder blue slacks before continuing, "Wildlife that islanders complain about: deer get into folks' gardens, raccoons kill chickens and get into trash, and beavers chop down trees and redirect streams."

Bear interrupted. "Wait a second! People were talking about shooting beavers at Mooney's Market!"

All three adults sat up straight and turned to Bear. "What? Who?"

"Two men, two women. They play tennis. One of them had a moustache like this." Bear gestured by circling his index fingers at the outer corners of his lips.

"Beau Burneside?"

"Is there another handlebar moustache on Oxbow Island?"

"Let's not jump to conclusions. I can't imagine that man shooting…" Sally Parker's voice trailed off.

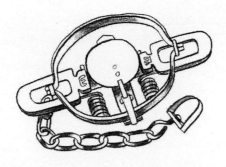

7

"Bear, is that what you were upset about?" His grandmother spoke quietly. "When you came back from the store, is that why you wanted to go for a walk, because you heard people talking about hurting beavers?"

Bear looked at her, shook his head, and tried to remember what he had been upset about. It seemed like weeks earlier, not an hour since he had returned from the store. When he remembered, he sunk back in his rocking chair and stared at the plate in his lap. He began haltingly. "No... it was worse." He reached down to stroke Honey's silky ears and thought of the beaver they had seen swimming in the pond that morning. "No. It wasn't worse." Watching Honey lick her injured paw, Bear realized there are worse things than being embarrassed. He sat up straight and told them about meeting Olivia in Mooney's Market.

He concluded, "I've never seen her before. How was I supposed to know she lives here? You'd think she was Mr. Mooney's daughter, the way he took her side." Bear swallowed loudly before continuing in a whisper, "I think Mr. Mooney hates me now." The adults sat in sympathetic silence. After a moment he was able to look at each of them and ask, "Who is this Olivia girl?"

They took turns explaining and correcting each other as they told the story of Olivia and her father, Victor Anaya. The father and daughter had arrived on the island before Olivia was school-aged. They could not agree on whether Olivia's mother was alive or had ever been seen on the island. Either way, Mrs. Frost and his grandmother agreed it was a sad sight, a young girl without a mother. The Anayas lived in a tidy one-story house on the south side of the island near the ball field and horse barns. Victor Anaya had been a well-respected roofer, strong and efficient. They marveled, recalling him carrying whole packages of heavy asphalt shingles, one on each shoulder, up ladders to the top of the tall, steep, roofs of Oxbow Island.

"No one worked harder or faster than that man," his grandmother began.

"A veritable muscle machine."

"And he never stopped to chitter-chat. Not that he was unfriendly. He would talk. He would even sing while walking on the peak of a roof. But he always kept working."

Mrs. Frost's face drooped with the weight of her memories. "You couldn't ask for a nicer fellow."

"He did all our roofs." Bear's grandmother said. "You've heard us talk about the roofer who was injured, fell from the roof of the market. Well, that was Victor Anaya, Olivia's father. Since he came back from the hospital in a wheelchair, they've kept to themselves.

The adults stared down at their hands, lost in their memories.

Bear looked from face to face, but no one made eye contact with him.

Mrs. Frost exhaled slowly. "I was at the market that day. It was lunchtime. The market was packed, everyone lined up for Wanda's lunch special." Mrs. Frost looked up at the clear blue sky and shook her head three times: *no, no, no.* "Victor never took a lunch break. 'Always work a full day,' he would say." The Professor and Bear's grandmother nodded their heads in solemn agreement. "Somebody screamed. The sound cut right through me. I can still hear it. We all raced out of the market and down to the shore, desperate to help but terrified to move him Mrs. Frost quietly blew her nose and wiped her eyes.

"Somehow, Olivia ended up there. I don't know if someone went and got her. I don't know. She shouldn't have been there. She saw it all. She couldn't have been more than six or seven at the time. Wearing a pretty little blue dress, her hair in long shiny black braids with white ribbons, she ran down the steep hill and pushed her way through the crowd. She never said a word, just gripped her father's hand as they carried his body to the helicopter. She climbed in after they loaded him and they flew to a hospital in Boston." Mrs. Frost stared at the road. "We all stood there. No one said a word even after the helicopter was out of sight. After a while, I walked home. Forgot my groceries in the market but I didn't go back for them. It was over a week before I could go back there."

After a long pause, his grandmother spoke. "He was gone for months, and Olivia too. I never heard where she went, who she stayed with.

"One day they returned. I remember everyone standing back so they could be the first ones off the ferry. People were clapping, but they were crying too. Victor was in a wheelchair and Olivia was pushing him. Her long hair cut short. That's when she started cutting her own hair. Her dad had always braided it." Bear's grandmother reached out to touch his unruly brown curls.

"After the accident, Olivia said she wanted to make it easier for her father, show him she could take care of him and herself too." She cleared her throat and brushed her long silvery hair out of her face. "It was a shock to see him in the wheelchair and Olivia with her hair chopped off. They both looked so serious, staring straight ahead while we were cheering and clapping. She wasn't a little girl anymore and he wasn't a young man either. They seemed old, ancient. It made me wonder what we were so happy about."

"He lived!" Bear said. "You were happy he lived."

"And they came home, dear." Mrs. Frost patted her neighbor's knee as she spoke.

"Until that day, it never occurred to me that every morning before Victor went to work that big tough man had brushed and braided his daughter's hair." His grandmother set her plate on the porch railing and rocked slowly in her rocking chair

The Professor continued the story. "All the island carpenters collaborated, constructing a ramp and other wheelchair accommodations for their home. We held fundraisers to assist with medical expenses, but after a few months, Victor let it be known that they were not in need of charity."

Mrs. Frost sat up straight and spoke forcefully, "We never thought of it as *charity*. It was just the right thing to do. We live on an island. Sooner or later we all need a little help from our neighbors. That's the island way. You share what you can and if trouble comes you accept what you need. That's the island way."

The others seemed amused by her words, knowing Mrs. Frost was always the first to refuse any and all assistance.

Sally Parker smiled at her neighbor. "Olivia does everything. That's why she's not in school. One of the teachers takes assignments to her, but she's done all her schoolwork at home since the accident. Mike Mooney helps them out any way he can. He was devastated by the accident. Not that it was his fault."

"He said, 'The hot dogs are on the house,'" Bear recalled.

The adults nodded.

"She had these weird mushrooms in her basket?"

"She gathers a lot of their food in the woods," his grandmother added. "I'm sure money is tight for them. Mushrooms can be poisonous, but Olivia knows more about them and other wild edibles than I ever will. She gathers all her basket-making materials and plants for dyeing them too."

"She makes baskets? Do you think she made the basket on her back?"

"I'm sure," his grandmother said. "She and her father work together. They sell them in the fancy craft shops in Portland."

A man in the road hollered, "Hello." All heads turned toward the stranger.

Only Honey greeted him. She limped across the yard and sat patiently at his feet with her tail wagging the dust off the dirt road. Her head tilted up expectantly.

"Who is the interloper with the unusual insurance policy?" the Professor murmured as they stood to acknowledge the twitchy, thin man nervously tapping his hand against his thigh.

Bear puzzled over the Professor's comment. The stranger's pants ballooned around his thin legs. A belt gathered the extra fabric at his waist and striped suspenders slipped precariously on his slouching shoulders. A man this thin with pants so large needed a belt and suspenders to hold up his pants. Bear smiled when he realized that was what the Professor meant by "insurance." The stranger gripped a clipboard in one hand and nervously tapped the bulging pocket above Honey's nose with the other.

"He looks like a scarecrow," Bear joked quietly.

"With a clipboard."

"In need of geographical guidance?"

The adults tried to hide their smiles.

Mrs. Frost was the first to remember her manners. "Do you need directions?" she asked kindly.

"Nope," the stranger replied with a sneer as he moved toward them with Honey walking close at his side. "Is this your dog?" The man's eyebrows jerked upward and disappeared behind his hair. Every strand on his head appeared to be combed forward, obscuring his forehead and now his eyebrows. Would his eyes be next to disappear behind the curtain of beige hair?

Bear hopped off the porch and began scratching the golden retriever's head. "She's my grandmother's. Her name's Honey the Wonder Dog because…" Bear looked at the man's expressionless face and decided against telling him more. "She's special. Come on, Honey."

When Honey didn't follow him, Bear took hold of her collar and pulled her back to the porch before signaling for Honey to sit. She plopped onto the floor with a deep, disappointed sigh.

"As I'm sure you know, there's a leash law in the city," the man said.

Mrs. Frost moved to the top of her porch steps and tapped her cane loudly against the floor. "Young man," she said to the stranger, who had to be at least fifty, "does this," she waved her cane toward the empty dirt road, "look like the city to you?"

He stood with his feet in a wide stance and his hands on his hips, looking up at the tiny woman. "Oxbow Island is part of the City of Portland, as I'm sure you know." His tone was insulting, suggesting she wasn't smart enough to know precisely where she had lived for the past nine decades.

Honey lifted her nose from the porch floor and stuck her head between Bear's legs, eyeing the stranger.

The Professor stepped in front of Mrs. Frost before speaking with ice in his voice. "I haven't had the pleasure of making your acquaintance, but I can assure you we are all aware of the municipal boundaries. Obviously, Honey"— at the mention of her name, the dog moved to sit in front of Bear—"is neither a menace to society nor running at large." The Professor turned to Mrs. Frost and gestured that she should be seated, but she clenched her cane and shook her head *no*.

The Professor's words had no impact on the stranger, who had begun writing on his clipboard.

Bear's grandmother joined the Professor and Mrs. Frost at the top of the stairs. "Excuse me, Mr...."

"Flood. Floyd Flood. I'm the animal control officer," he said, without looking up from his writing. "What's the address here?"

"Mr. Flood," she began, her voice vibrating with an anger Bear had never heard before, "my dog is on private property and is not bothering anyone. We can all agree that the leash law was intended for nuisance dogs that are a threat to others. As anyone can see," she gestured to Honey who was watching the stranger warily, "that's not the case here." Her voice rose and she leaned further forward with each word.

The fur rose between Honey's shoulders in response to her owner's anger. There was a low rumble in her throat.

For the first time, Mr. Flood looked at them and smiled. Perhaps he was a reasonable man. "Yes, she's on the porch now, looking like a good dog, but a few minutes ago she charged me in the street as I was walking by. The little boy had to drag her off by the collar." He tapped his pen against the form on his clipboard. "It's all in the report."

Little boy, Bear fumed. The blonde woman in front of Mooney's Market had called him a *rude little boy*. When would it stop? With his fists clenched, he joined the adults and Honey at the top of the porch steps and glared down at Floyd Flood.

"The fine is forty-five dollars for the first offense. Doubles to ninety if you don't pay within a week. So it's best not to be irresponsible."

"Irresponsible?" Bear's grandmother took a step down the stairs toward the animal control officer. "Irresponsible?" Her voice rose as she took another step.

Mrs. Frost reached out with her cane and hooked it around her neighbor's forearm. When his grandmother glanced back, Viola Frost shook her head in warning and gently tugged on the cane restraining Sally Parker's right arm.

From her shoulders to the base of her tail, Honey's fur was pointing to the sky as Bear and the adults glared at Floyd Flood. He laid the ticket on the bottom porch step, turned and walked down the dirt road. No one spoke until he turned the corner at the end of Maple Street.

"Oh, my." Mrs. Frost was shaking as she moved toward her chair, but it was anger and not unsteadiness that caused the tremors. "What an unpleasant man."

"Unpleasant?" the Professor boomed as he assisted her to her seat. "Abhorrent, distasteful, irksome, obnoxious, and repellent are the words I would use to describe that bilious cartoon villain."

"I thought you were going to hit him." Bear's brown eyes were wide with awe as he spoke to his grandmother.

"I'm sorry to say that I wanted to. I'm afraid I'm not much of a role model."

"Good thing I stopped you or they'd be hauling you off to the hoosegow," Mrs. Frost teased.

Everyone seemed to relax as they settled into their chairs and rocked slowly.

"It appears that a lack of impulse control runs in the family," the Professor said.

"You don't know the half of it," his grandmother said. "When Bear's mother was eleven, she got in a snowball fight with her cousin that ended with—."

"Mom got in a fight?" Bear interrupted.

His grandmother placed her index finger over her pursed lips. "It was nothing. Really."

"The apple doesn't fall far from the tree," Mrs. Frost said with a smile.

"Bear." His grandmother looked intently at him. "Was Honey on her leash when she got caught in that trap?"

Bear felt the blood drain from his face. Was it his fault that Honey had been hurt? "Oh," he groaned as he reached to hug her dog.

His grandmother blinked and slowly nodded her head. His expression was answer enough.

"Now, don't you boys have some wood to stack?" Mrs. Frost blurted with forced enthusiasm.

The Professor and Honey jumped up. Was she trying to prove she hadn't been hurt? Bear slunk behind them. This had already been the longest day of his life and now he had to stack wood. He groaned, but nobody noticed.

"Come with me, young lad," the Professor said. "We will strategize while we stack. My analytical faculties are always strengthened by manual labor."

Bear shook his head and followed the oversized man who was loping toward the pile of firewood that had been dumped in his yard.

As usual, the Professor continued talking even when it appeared that no one was listening. The words drifted back to Bear. "The way I see it, we have two challenges. First, we must identify the person who is indiscriminately and illegally placing traps on our island. Second, we need to plot a suitable revenge for Mr. Floyd Flood. He has besmirched the reputation of Honey the Wonder Dog."

Bear ran to catch up with the Professor when he heard the word "revenge."

8

On Sunday morning, Bear awoke to the smell of pancakes and bacon cooking. He raced downstairs with Honey trotting at his heals. She showed no sign of the previous day's injury. He hoped his grandmother had put blueberries in the pancakes and heated the syrup. There is nothing worse than cold syrup on your pancakes. "Keeps the butter from melting," he explained to Honey as they both leapt over the last two steps and collided in a pile by the front door.

"Good morning, Buckaroo Bear!" his grandmother said cheerfully ignoring their crash landing.

"Blueberry pancakes!" Bear checked the stove top. "And Mickey Mouse too! You made Mickey Mouse pancakes!" He was delighted to see the perfectly round pancake head combined with two smaller pancake "ears."

"Wouldn't be Sunday without Mickey Mouse and the color comics." She gestured toward Bear's seat at the table, where the newspaper funny pages were waiting for him. "The Professor and I were talking," she said as she placed Bear's breakfast in front of him. "We decided that you deserve the day off. Nobody goes to school seven days a week, and yesterday was very…productive. I thought we could go into Portland for a movie and lunch or—"

"No time for that. I've got too much to do." Bear poured the warm syrup on his pancakes before taking a sweet bite and grinning up at his grandmother.

She sat down across from him and waited.

"Can we bake cookies? I owe Mrs. Frost some and I thought I could take some to Olivia and her dad too." Bear took another bite before continuing. "You know, to apologize for yesterday." The truth was, while stacking wood with the Professor, Bear had developed a plan for catching the poaching trapper.

"That's very nice." Sally Parker reached across the table to pat her grandson's hand as she nodded her approval. "What are we baking? I can run to Mooney's Market while you finish breakfast."

Bear was uncertain. Mrs. Frost preferred his oatmeal raisin cookies with dried apricots and walnuts. But Olivia was a kid like him, and he loved his peanut butter chocolate chip cookies. That was his favorite of all the recipes that he and his grandmother had perfected over the years. But Olivia was a mushroom eater. Maybe she didn't like kid things. She wasn't like most kids. Besides, she might not agree to help him no matter how good the cookies were. He decided to go with the sure thing and make Mrs. Frost happy by making oatmeal raisin cookies.

As soon as she left the house, Bear grabbed his notebook and began to make a list. There was no reason for his grandmother to know everything he did. If he was going to catch whoever was setting traps on the island, he needed help from someone who had been born in this century. His grandmother, Mrs. Frost, and the Professor were kind, thoughtful people, but Olivia knew the woods better than they did and she was not afraid of anyone or anything. He had to persuade her to help him.

An hour later, Bear was at Mrs. Frost's front door with a plate of warm cookies. The sight of her grinning wrinkled face and twinkling eyes when she met him at the door made him stand a little taller.

"Come in. Come in. I smelled those before I heard you knock." She lifted a cookie off the plate as he stepped over the threshold. "I don't suppose you have time to help a little old lady with a new puzzle?"

Bear was eager to get to Olivia's house as soon as possible, but he was also afraid that she might still be mad about how he had treated her in the grocery store. And he knew that if he said "No, I have to go," Mrs. Frost would be polite and understanding, but her smile would shrink a little and her shoulders would sag. Bear did not want to be reminded of how old and frail his friend was. The trip to Olivia's house would have to wait a little longer.

"I love puzzles. What're you doing? Hope it's not all white or something crazy like that."

"State of Maine. I can't even get the silly box open." She shook her head and held up her crooked arthritic fingers. "Bear, you have to promise me that you will never get old. It's a horrible thing to feel so helpless."

Bear had no idea how to respond, so he went to the kitchen for a knife and carefully sliced the plastic wrap. Together they sat on the folding chairs at the card table by the window. Bear's youthful nimble fingers picked up the pieces that were upside down and turned them over. Mrs. Frost slid all of the edge pieces to one corner of the table, grouping them by color.

"There's a lot of green and it's all the same shade," Bear said.

"I know." Mrs. Frost sounded excited by the challenge. "I've been thinking about that trap. We have to assume that if there's one trap, there are more," she said, without looking up from sorting puzzle pieces. Bear was surprised that he and his ninety-year-old friend had reached the same conclusion, but he didn't say a word. "It must have been set by someone who lives near where Honey was injured."

Bear kept flipping pieces. "Maybe. I hadn't thought of that."

"What we need to do is go to each of the summer properties on that pond and near the brook and check for traps along the water's edge. I have a list of suspects, including the Burnesides. I checked with Gus this morning, when he brought the paper. He knows which ones are closed up for the season and which ones have caretakers lurking about. I put stars next to the cottages that are safe to check. Gus can update us each day. We don't want anyone checking an estate if there's a man with a gun on the property."

Bear shivered at the thought and remembered the two couples in front of the market joking about shooting beavers. "Where's the list?"

She gestured toward the dining room table.

The list was long and thorough. Gus knew all the summer people on his paper route. When they stopped delivery, he knew they had closed up their home for the season. Checking those properties might work.

Yesterday, the Professor had told him that they should have an educational seminar for the island's residents on coexisting with wildlife. The Professor thought the problem was a lack of education. He also wanted to call the city and report Floyd Flood, the animal control officer, for unprofessional conduct.

It seemed that everyone had a plan. But Bear liked his plan the best: he and Olivia would build tree houses around the hidden pond. They could camp out in the tree tops, waiting to catch whoever was setting the traps and then dump red paint on him. That way he would be easy to identify if he got away from them.

Mrs. Frost looked at him eagerly, waiting for his response.

"Maybe. It might work." She seemed dejected, so he added, "Thanks for this list." He folded it up and put it in his pants pocket.

When all of the puzzle pieces were right side up and sorted by color, Bear returned to his grandmother's house for the next plate of cookies, Honey the Wonder Dog, and directions for finding the Anayas' house.

"Bear, you have to promise me you'll keep Honey on a leash. It's not just that horrible Flood man. There could be more traps. It's for her safety. Do you understand?"

Bear nodded. "I promise, Gramma. Really, I do."

Bear took the South Loop Trail. At the sound of rushing water he paused, examined the ground for traps, and stepped off the path. Behind a clump of prickly wild raspberry bushes he found the gushing water. Someone had done their best to tear down a beaver dam. Twigs and branches were mounded on both sides of the brook as it gushed through the newly created opening.

"That trap must have been meant for a beaver," he whispered to Honey as he looked around to see if they were alone. "Let's get out of here."

A short while later, he smelled horse manure and turned left onto a path covered with pine needles. The lack of roots and rocks on this part of the trail surprised him. There weren't many smooth footpaths on the island. When he stepped out of the woods they were at the back of the horse barns. Bear looked at Honey and looked at the map his grandmother had drawn. Honey seemed as confused as he was.

"Says to walk beside the barn then go right toward the ball field."

Honey ambled forward with Bear close behind. The ball field was easy to see from the front of the barn, but he was disoriented. He had never approached the ball field from this side before. Still, it was shorter than following the road around the outside of the island.

"We got this: cross the ball field, turn right on a dirt road, it's the only house."

Bear found what used to be a driveway. Nobody had driven there in years: the grass was long and wild flowers filled the ruts where tires used to press them down. Norway maples with bittersweet twining up their trunks leaned in over the narrow opening. Bear and Honey looked down the overgrown tunnel. At the far end, a truck covered with a blue tarp filled the opening, blocking their view. It was impossible to see what lay beyond.

Slowly, cautiously, Bear and Honey moved forward. Bear gripped the plate of cookies with one hand and Honey's leash with the other. When they reached the truck's rear bumper they could hear a man singing in a low voice, but the words were unrecognizable. They crept beside the vehicle, deliberately, quietly, curious to see who was singing. Boy and dog stepped in front of the truck and peered across a tidy yard surrounded by raised garden beds. A small blue house was at the far edge. Olivia stood at a picnic table with her back to them. Bear peered toward the house but couldn't see the source of the music.

Suddenly a shrill, high-pitched sound interrupted the singing. Bear gasped, startled by the noise. He lurched backward, clutching the cookies to his chest, and collided with the truck.

Olivia turned toward the commotion. Bear froze in place, unsure what he was seeing. He gulped for air, blinked, and looked closely to make sure he was right. The front of her shirt was covered with blood. A long thin knife was in her right hand. At the sight of Bear and Honey, she waved the knife in the air.

Bear's head filled with the voice of Mr. Mooney: "You are lucky she didn't hit you. She's got a mean right cross."

Bear screamed, dropped the cookies, and ran as fast as he could with Honey at his side. Before they reached the back of the truck, he heard a man holler, "Run! Catch him!"

Bear's heart pounded. He pumped his arms and lifted his legs, struggling for speed, but he could hear her foot falls. He made it to the opening for the ball field. Had he ever run this far this fast before? At home plate he could hear her breathing. Before he reached first base, he felt a hand grab the back of his T-shirt's collar. His shoulders jerked backwards and he struggled to keep his feet beneath him. He failed and fell to the ground with a thump.

Trapped, he dropped Honey's leash so she could run to safety. If Honey ran home without him, his grandmother would know to send help. Bear curled into a ball and wrapped his arms around his head, protecting himself from the blows he expected to come. He could see her muddy boots. Bear's head filled with the sound of his jagged breaths.

"What're you doing?" Olivia asked.

Slowly, he uncovered his face and looked up. Honey was sitting beside him, happily wagging her tail.

"You run faster than I would've expected," she said.

Bear sat up and stared at Olivia's blood-stained shirt, and then checked her hands for weapons. "You don't have a knife?"

"Knife? No, I'd never run with a knife. You could hurt yourself."

"Well, yeah, I know that," he mumbled.

"I saw you brought cookies." Olivia laughed. "Course they're on the ground now." She waited for an explanation.

As they stood there looking at each other his terror evaporated, replaced by embarrassment.

"Well, I thought…" His voice faded.

"Come back to our house. We can try those cookies, if the birds haven't eaten them all. I told my dad about you. He wants to meet you and talk about the lady's slippers being dug up. Truth is we don't get a lot of company. I think he's lonely."

Bear was surprised by her chattiness and struggled to think of something to say as they walked toward the overgrown driveway. "My grandmother and I made the cookies," he began, and then remembered why he was there. "I wanted to apologize."

Olivia waved away his words. "No, no. My dad and I've been talking. We need to find out who took those plants. I'm glad you told me about it."

That was nice of her to suggest he had *told her about it,* rather than saying he had accused her, in the middle of Mooney's Market. Olivia's friendliness increased Bear's shame about how he had treated her. He stopped walking. He had to apologize fully. She deserved it. As he searched for the right words he noticed the blood, splattered on the front of her shirt, on her hands, and even a spot on the side of her nose. "So…what were you doing with that knife?"

She looked down at her shirt, the same green-and-gray plaid one she had worn the day before, and laughed. "Is that what scared you?"

Bear struggled to appear calm.

"I went fishing this morning. Caught two stripers. Now I'm cleaning them." She said this as if it were the most normal thing in the world.

For her it was, Bear realized. She smelled like a freshly opened can of tuna.

"We have a bigger problem than the lady's slippers," Bear confided. Olivia stopped walking and looked at him. "I think someone's trapping beavers."

9

"Welcome!" Victor Anaya shouted across the yard as Olivia and Bear bent to pick up the oatmeal raisin cookies that were scattered in the Anayas' driveway.

"My dad. He thinks he's funny. Just warning you," Olivia said.

"I heard that!" Victor Anaya sat in front of them. He had soundlessly rolled his wheelchair across the yard in less time than it had taken them to pick up the cookies.

"Hey, how'd you do that?" Bear asked as he examined the wheelchair. "You're fast and silent!"

Victor reached out his hand. It was the size of a dinner plate. "Hi, I'm Olivia's dad, Victor Anaya, and I really am funny. Punny, actually." He chuckled at his joke.

"Bear." They shook hands, Bear's hand disappearing inside Victor's strong grasp.

"I know who you are. Olivia, can you shut off the radio and get some apple cider too?"

Olivia ran ahead to the house.

"On Sundays I like to sing a little opera along with the radio. Italian, German, I have no idea what I'm saying, but it sure feels good." Honey sat with her head in Victor's lap as he stroked her ears. "Do you sing?"

Bear shook his head and studied Olivia's father. It was hard to see beyond his magnetic smile. His arms and chest bulged with muscles like a superhero in a movie. Bear had been expecting to see a broken man, but Victor Anaya looked like a bodybuilder.

"What's your dog's name?"

"Honey the Wonder Dog."

"She must be special. Sounds pawsome." Victor laughed at his pun.

When they reached the picnic table, Bear set his cookies next to the two large fish that Olivia had caught. At the opposite end of the table were wooden ovals and a power drill.

"You were drilling. Singing and drilling." Bear remembered the sounds that had scared him when he first arrived at the Anayas' house.

"Yup, basket bottoms," Victor said, and held up one of the ovals, which had holes drilled around its outer edge. "Could you tell the difference between the singing and the drilling?" He continued without waiting for an answer. "We use these for the bottoms of some of our baskets. Olivia does the basket weaving and I make the bottoms and sew the liners. I call it team work. She," he gestured toward Olivia, who was carrying two glasses of apple cider, "calls it child labor."

Olivia shook her head and rolled her eyes as she set the glasses down and joined Bear and her father at the picnic table.

"What brings you here?" Victor asked.

"Oh, it's a long story. I got in trouble at school and they sent me to my grandmother's."

"I bet you grabbed some girl," Olivia teased.

"No!" Bear attempted to defend himself. "I shoved a guy and he bumped into the teacher and they both fell over."

"Why?" Olivia asked.

"He called me 'Baby Bear,' okay, and I hate to be called Baby Bear."

This made Olivia laugh.

"I meant," Victor said, "what brings you here, to our home, today?" Victor looked back and forth between Olivia and Bear. "As for the nickname, I like it. It's funny, like an inside joke between friends. Anyone can see you're going to grow up to be a giant grizzly of a man."

Bear sat up straight, reached over the dead fish for a cookie, and smiled.

"You know, I have nicknames for your gang," Victor said.

"My gang?"

"Gang, band, clan, tribe, people. You pick the word." Victor gestured with his hand that the term was unimportant. "I call them the Professor, the Puzzler, and the Baker. That's your grandmother. After my accident the three of them would come wandering in every Sunday with a pie, a puzzle, or a story to tell. They would not leave me alone. Made me feel helpless after a while."

"Really?" Bear said, not sure if Victor Anaya was joking or complaining.

"They didn't tell you? I thought maybe they sent you."

Bear shook his head, but Victor seemed skeptical.

"I came because I wanted to apologize to Olivia. And ask her for her help. I didn't tell my grandmother that last part."

Victor and Olivia leaned forward and waited for him to explain.

"You know the woods better than I do. Yesterday Honey got caught in a trap. I heard a guy with a moustache talking about shooting beavers, and today I saw where someone had torn down a beaver dam. If we build some tree houses near beaver dams or where we find more traps, we can sit there on guard duty. When the trapper comes back, kaboom, we dump red paint on him."

Olivia nodded her approval. Bear and Olivia began talking over each other, bursting with ideas for water balloons, rope slides, rotten produce, and deep pits filled with fire ants.

"I see a few problems with this plan," Victor interrupted. "If moustache man is the poacher, he has a gun. You don't throw water balloons at a man with a gun. Do you have any other ideas?"

Bear felt deflated. "My neighbors do, but they're—not to be mean, but they're old."

Victor raised his eyebrows.

Bear looked at Olivia for guidance but she looked away.

Victor gently scolded, "Being old beats the alternative. If you're lucky you'll get to be old someday too. Compared to Mrs. Frost I'm young." He picked up three wooden ovals and began juggling them. "Compared to you I'm old. It's all relative."

Victor grinned like a little boy as he threw the basket bottoms higher and higher in the air. Bear doubted that anyone could look at this man juggling in the sunshine and see him as old. And then one piece sailed out of reach and he let the other two crash to the ground.

Victor shrugged. "What're their ideas?"

"The Professor says we should put up informational posters and have an educational program on coexisting with wildlife. He would. I mean, he's a professor. Mrs. Frost says it's probably a summer person. She thinks they're to blame for everything that's wrong on the island: high prices, long lines, too much traffic." Bear remembered the list in his pocket, pulled it out, and placed it on the picnic table. "She wants us to check the properties of people near the trap Honey stepped in yesterday.

Victor reached for the list. "Between the three of you, I'd say you have a complete strategy. You've thought of everything and that, my young friend, is the benefit of working together. May I help too, or is it just Olivia you want? I can build platforms for the tree houses. But no dumping paint on people and no fire ants. You want to identify the suspect, not get shot. Okay?" He looked at both of them.

Sitting at the picnic table, they made a list and assigned jobs to everyone. They all agreed that Bear's grandmother and Honey should search the summer people's properties. If anyone confronted her about being on private property, she could pretend to be innocently walking her dog. Bear planned to return the next morning at eight o'clock sharp so he and Olivia could get an early start. They needed to catch the poacher before any more animals were hurt.

"Thanks for your help," Bear said when he stood to leave.

"It's nice to be asked." Victor's face was solemn for the first time. "After my accident, everyone wanted to help us. I knew their intentions were kind, but it hurt after a while. Most people just see the wheelchair." He tapped the arm rests on his chair. "They don't see me." Victor Anaya looked into Bear's eyes and said, "You're the first person in six years who's asked us for help. That's a special type of kindness."

Olivia reached down to rub Honey's belly as the golden retriever stretched out on her back and Bear clipped the leash on Honey's collar. He would keep her safe and avoid getting another ticket from Floyd Flood today.

Bear decided to take a detour before returning to his grandmother's. He wanted to get another look at Beau Burneside. Hoping to spy on him at the Tennis Club, Bear took Water Street past the island's small business district and turned onto Club Road. At the far end of the fenced-in tennis courts Bear stopped, remembering they had called him a "rude little boy" the day before. He didn't want to be seen, but he needed to know: were these the type of people who would hurt Honey or any other animal? Everyone at the club was dressed in white. Would he even be able to recognize them?

On the opposite side of the furthest court, a trim tan man was bouncing a ball on his tennis racquet. Even seeing him from behind, Bear knew it was Beau Burneside. Short, bald Pierce Calhoun faced Burneside, looking bored—but not as bored as their wives, who sat rigidly, silently on Adirondack chairs behind their husbands. For all of their money, they didn't appear to be enjoying themselves. Studying the two couples in their bright white clothing, Bear could not imagine any of them on a trail in the woods. He didn't like the Calhouns and the Burnesides, but they didn't seem like poachers.

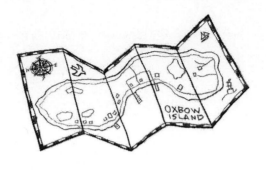

10

Bear was feeling grumpy as he and Honey went downstairs for breakfast Monday morning. The plan he and the Anayas had put together had received mixed reviews. His grandmother and the Professor were concerned that he had forgotten why he was on Oxbow Island, and he had school work that he was expected to complete. He could not change his schedule on a whim. Bear had assumed they were committed to catching the poacher, but apparently he was wrong. Mrs. Frost had tried to take Bear's side, but they wouldn't even listen to her. His grandmother had reminded her and Bear that it was impulsive behavior that led to this problem in the first place. Bear had tried to reason with them. What was the difference between making a map for them and locating traps and dams? But they remained convinced that he had to finish one assignment before he started the next one.

The Professor and his grandmother were talking in the living room. Bear and Honey slowed with each step down the stairs before coming to a complete stop on the bottom tread. They stood in silence for a minute before his grandmother spoke.

"C'mon, Buckaroo, there's no need to be grumpy. You just have to get some work done for the Professor and then you can meet up with Olivia. Work first, play later. You know the rules."

"A human being must have occupation if he or she is not to become a nuisance to the world." The Professor looked over the top of his glasses as he spoke.

There were days when Bear was amused by the tall professor's way of speaking. Today was not one of them. He was supposed to meet Olivia in fifteen minutes. It was urgent that they catch the poacher before another animal was injured or, worse, killed. There was no time for lectures. He had thought his grandmother and the Professor would understand that better than anyone else. Bear had been wrong.

"Speaking of nuisance," Bear said with anger in each word. "Yesterday, Victor Anaya told me about you."

Their looks registered the surprise he had hoped for. "He said you would go over there every Sunday and look down on him because he's in a wheelchair."

His grandmother reacted as if she had been slapped. The smile disappeared from her face. She pulled her head back and glanced toward the Professor.

"Oh, no," she said, shaking her head. "No. We never. Why?"

The Professor cleared his throat. "I am confident that you know your grandmother's character. A statement such as that does not warrant a response." Bear looked at the Professor's stern face and then his grandmother's. All the color had drained from her cheeks. Her lips were pulled into a short thin line. He matched the Professor's stern look and crossed his arms in front of his chest. When Honey left Bear's side to lay her head in his grandmother's lap with a quiet whimper, Bear's heart ached, but he knew he was right. Olivia was waiting for him. They were running out of time.

"You will complete your mapping assignment this morning," the Professor said. He looked at his neighbor and friend, but Sally was looking down, petting her dog. The Professor continued, "You'll be on your own today. Honey will accompany your grandmother."

His grandmother was still.

"She's going to the Ward and Duncan estates. Gus said the owners have departed for the season. He isn't aware of a caretaker at either property. Come home for lunch. This afternoon, we will conclude our wood stacking."

His grandmother laid her head on Honey's neck, seeming to whisper to the dog. Bear tried to assess her mood, but her long hair concealed her face.

"Is that clear?" The Professor looked at Bear's grandmother and Honey when he spoke.

But Bear knew who he was talking to. "Yeah."

Bear reached for the door knob. As he pulled the door open he paused, expecting his grandmother to say, "Wait, you haven't had your breakfast yet." Nothing. Not a word. He kept moving forward, picking up speed.

Once he was on Maple Street he began to jog, going right past Mrs. Frost's without even a glance to see if she was in the window waving at him. He realized he didn't have his backpack. He didn't have his notebook. He didn't have any snacks. It was too late to go back to the house. He couldn't face his grandmother and the Professor again. He had to go to Olivia's.

When he arrived at the woodpecker tree on the edge of the woods, he focused on running soundlessly, rolling through each step with silent footfalls. If they were going to catch the poacher, Bear would have to become quicker and quieter. He needed to train. Plus, he would need to be able to keep up with Olivia. He was tired of having to stop and catch his breath. Bear struggled to find a pace he could maintain as he hopped over tree roots, eased around large rocks, and ducked under low branches. He startled a mourning dove in the brush beside the trail. The bird took flight, calling *coo, coo, coo* as it departed. Bear kept his focus on the trail and on his breathing, silently jogging through the woods. The bird's calls faded in the distance.

Bear stopped. There was a trap on the trail. A shredded carcass was still attached. Slowly he knelt and saw the mangled remains of a beaver. The broad flat tail and a webbed rear foot remained, but most of the body had been eaten by another animal. Stuck in the trap, the beaver would have been defenseless. Had the injured beaver been dragged here by a predator? Bear knelt to gently lift the beaver's remains with the trap attached to a front foot. He carried them off the path and laid them on a thick bed of moss before gathering rocks to pile on the corpse. The least he could do was protect the beaver from other scavengers.

When he finally appeared in the Anaya's yard, Olivia greeted him. "Hey, you're late."

"Would you like some wood?" Victor waved a two-by-four and smiled at his joke as he called out to Bear. "I started these yesterday after you left. I have the boards cut for four platforms but I need the exact measurements of the trees before I can finish them. Measure twice, cut once, I always say." Victor stopped talking when he saw Bear's expression. "What's wrong?"

With as few words as possible, Bear told them about the dead trapped beaver.

"We'd better get to work," Victor said.

Olivia and Bear stood by the picnic table while Victor Anaya sat at his table saw. The wood was neatly sorted beside him in four small piles. Each stack had three short two-by-fours for the structure and five boards that were shorter than Bear. He recalled the tree house he had made with Devi and Jasmine that summer. They'd used more lumber for one wall than Victor had on the ground around him.

"They're kind of small."

"Everyone's a critic," Victor said as he turned the saw off. "Hey, I never promised you a palace in the sky." He rubbed his hands on his pants before grabbing a rag to wipe off his table saw. "You two have to carry them into the woods and lift them into place. I figured small was the way to go. You can sit with your back against the tree trunk and your legs hanging down. Should be comfortable enough."

Bear's mind raced, estimating the distance to where Honey had been trapped. It had to be over a mile. That was a long way to carry something this awkward. Suddenly the platforms seemed gigantic. Victor could not help them like his father had when they'd built the tree house in his backyard this past summer. The trail was too rough for his wheelchair to navigate and he couldn't climb a tree. Bear looked at Olivia to see if she was feeling more confident than he was. The usual calm expression was on her face.

"Find your locations, where there's a trap or a dam. Then look in that area for a tree with branches that can support you. It could be a cluster of trees each with a diameter of at least a foot. You're going to measure the span at the height where the platform sits: how wide and long the platform needs to be. Make sense?"

Bear nodded as Olivia picked up a note pad, measuring tape, and pencil. He hoped she knew what her dad was talking about.

"It's possible you won't be able to climb up to measure if there aren't any low branches. Estimate the size and jot it down if you think we need a ladder, rope, or boards on the tree. Sketch each one and make a note if you're going to need braces for support. Get this done this morning and you can put them in place this afternoon. Got it?"

When they nodded, he grinned and said, "Scram! Get out of here. I don't have all day."

As Bear and Olivia loped through the Anayas' yard they heard the buzzing of the saw start up again.

"I didn't get half of what your dad said."

"No worries. We've built enough things together. I know what he needs."

They ran silently past the horse barn with Olivia in the lead. Bear thought about his father as they ran from the south side of the island toward the woodpecker tree. Karl

Houtman was just as cheerful as Victor and had a similar sense of humor. Of course, he couldn't sing opera or juggle. Whenever Bear needed something, his dad was always eager to help make it or fix it, just like Victor. Bear had convinced himself that he, Jasmine, and Devi had made their tree house. Now, he realized their dads had done most of the construction and planning. Yes, the kids had pounded the occasional nail and carried boards up and down the tree, but it was really the fathers' tree house. Olivia worked with Victor. She had to. They were a team. Bear envied that.

As they crossed the long log bridge, Bear said, "The path to the hidden pond is around the bend and there's a stream flowing out of it not far from the trail."

Several minutes later they stepped off the trail and slowed to a cautious walk, scanning the ground for traps. They followed the sound of rushing water as they picked their way through a grove of quaking aspen. The leaves flickered in the gentle breeze. Staring at the ground, they noticed scattered wood chips circling a tree, and then a metal trap. Olivia threw her arms out but Bear had already stopped and was reaching for a branch. He pushed his way past Olivia and jammed the branch into the trap. The jaws slammed shut.

"Wow! You weren't kidding," Olivia said.

As they stepped forward they could see another dam had been partially removed. Twigs, branches, and mud had been scraped off the top and water was cascading over the remaining mound.

"With all the twigs and branches close to the water, the beavers can rebuild this in a night," Olivia said. "The rushing water will let them know there's work to do."

Among the thin-limbed, greenish-white aspen saplings was one substantial red maple with branches sturdy enough to support a tree stand. Olivia quickly climbed up with her measuring tape and shouted numbers down to Bear, who carefully drew and noted the dimensions. When she finished, she turned to look toward the pond. "I can see the Burneside and Calhoun estates from here. Duncan and Ward too. They're all neighbors on the other side of the pond." She gestured toward the large ornate houses on the other side of the pond. Each one was surrounded by manicured gardens and unblemished lawns that were only enjoyed for a month or two each summer.

"Gramma's going to the Duncan and Ward properties today to look for traps. Gus says they've left for the season," Bear said as Olivia dropped down from the tree.

"Your grandmother has to assume Beau Burneside really does have a gun," Olivia said.

Bear nodded his agreement. No one could go near that estate until the owners had left the island.

"Let's follow the stream's edge. If we walk a few feet apart we might find more traps," Olivia said.

"Be careful. Those traps hurt," Bear said. "Just ask Honey."

They continued in silence until Bear noticed an area where the ground had been swept clean of leaf litter and twigs. Four palm-sized holes had been dug alongside a rotting log. "Olivia, you have to see this." He dropped to his knees. "I bet there were lady's slippers here."

"What if it's the same person?" Olivia asked. "We're off the main trail. You wouldn't find these," she touched the divots, "unless you were looking for something else."

Bear knew she was right. With a renewed sense of urgency, they continued their search for traps. The one Honey had tripped at the edge of the pond had been replaced. They quickly found a suitable tree near that spot and Olivia scrambled up to take the measurements. Halfway along the pond they decided to place another tree stand.

At the far end where a small stream flowed into the hidden pond they chose an oak tree for their fourth platform. Olivia climbed the tree and got Bear's attention. "I can see the Calhouns' and the Burnesides' houses from here." She looked back across the pond. "I think there's a beaver lodge that's been damaged between their properties." Olivia squinted toward the pond. "Maybe it's a brush pile. I wish I had my binoculars." She turned back to the pond. "Hey, they're playing croquet."

"Who?"

"At the Calhouns'. I see the bald guy and someone else. The croquet court is right on the edge of the pond. One wicket's practically in the water."

Olivia got back to work measuring and relaying the dimensions to Bear on the ground. When she was finished, she looked across the pond again. "Hah, one of the croquet balls went into the pond. They're trying to get it out without getting wet," she said, chuckling, before dropping to the ground.

"I never guessed we could see their homes from up there," Bear said as they jogged back to Olivia's house. "We can use the tree stands to guard the trail and spy on the estates. Bonus!"

11

When they returned to the Anayas' home, they were tired and hungry but eager to start building.

"We have to get those up today, Dad," Olivia said as she burst into the yard.

"We found more traps. I think a lodge's been damaged. And more lady's slippers have been dug up." Bear looked to Victor for reassurance.

"Give me your drawings and measurements." Victor glanced at the paper before speaking again. "Run on inside and get lunch while I work."

By the time they had finished eating, Victor had the first platform ready for them. A metal bar had been attached to each arm rest on his wheelchair, extending them in front of him. The platform was strapped to the bars above his lap.

Balanced on top were smaller loose boards for bracing and ladder steps up the tree.

"I can carry it part way," Victor answered Bear's unspoken question. The fully loaded wheelchair made a tight circle turn and Victor rolled rapidly away from them. Every muscle in his arms bulged, reminding Bear that the gliding movement was not as effortless as it appeared. "We've made improvements to the first stretch of the path, but we have a long way to go before I can get around the woods in this chair," he shouted over his shoulder.

Bear and Olivia grabbed the tool box and ran to catch up with Victor. Down the road, across the ball field, beside the horse barn, and across the pine needle path, Olivia and Bear jogged behind Victor's fast, fluid movement. The pine needles were silent and fragrant as if freshly placed. Bear realized that the Anayas must have improved this section of the trail.

"Okay kids, you're going to have to carry it from here," Victor said at the base of a boulder on the South Loop Trail. He spun his chair around to face them. "The rest of the trail's too rough for me."

Victor headed back as Olivia and Bear struggled to balance the toolbox and loose boards on top of the platform. At first they tried walking side by side with the platform between them. As they clambered over rocks, the loose items slid back and forth, crashing into their forearms.

When the trail narrowed they were forced to walk single file. Bear went first, walking backwards. Within minutes he tripped over a root and fell to the ground like a sack of potatoes. A sharp rock jabbed into his back and his head bounced off another. When the platform landed on his chest, the wood and tool box slid down and smashed into his chin. He lay pinned to the ground, feeling every ache and pain as Olivia scrambled to uncover him.

When everything was neatly stacked beside him, she turned to see Bear still lying flat on his back. "Are you all right?"

"Yeah." He slowly rolled to his side before sitting up and brushing the dirt off the back of his head and hands. He was in no hurry to pick up the platform again. When he was finally upright, he slowly brushed off the back of his pants before staring at the pile of wood for their first tree stand.

"I'll go first and carry it behind me," Olivia said. After a moment of silence she offered, "We can slow down a little."

"We're almost to the first trap and dam." Bear tried to muster some hope. He rubbed the back of his head with his right hand and then examined the blood on his fingers. He wiped his chin with the back of his left hand and the stinging caused him to wince.

"We should go to the trap that's farthest away first."

Bear groaned, his shoulders drooped and his mouth hung open as he stared at her.

"You do the hardest things first," she said as she stepped in front of the freshly loaded platform. "That way, when we're tired we'll just have the easy stuff left." She squatted down with her hands behind her and prepared to lift their load.

Bear wanted to scream *I'm tired now* but the determined look on her face stopped him. He bent down to pick up his end and felt the pain in his back.

"Slow and steady. We can do this," Olivia said and the words echoed in his head as they moved past each marked location.

At the far end of the hidden pond, they dropped the pile on the ground, stretched their arms and backs, and studied the oak tree.

"Three boards up for a ladder." Olivia seemed to be speaking to herself, talking through the plan they had agreed to that morning.

"Put the platform on that branch." Bear added.

"Yeah, then a brace on each side."

"We got this." A grin spread across Bear's face. He saw that Olivia was smiling too. Then he looked back at the pile of wood. "Getting the platform up will be hard," he realized.

Olivia kneeled beside the tool box. She pulled out some rope and a pulley and her grin widened. "Dad thought of everything."

By the time they had the first platform firmly attached to the tree, Bear had forgotten his aching muscles. They stepped back to examine their work. "Looks good," he said, sounding surprised.

Bear turned to Olivia, reaching out with his fist. Hesitatingly, she tapped her knuckles against his. "Kaboom!" Bear said before pulling his hand back, opening his fist and waggling his fingers at her.

Olivia looked at him and shook her head before starting to jog back to her house for the next platform. "One down," Olivia shouted back at Bear, "three to go and they're all easier than that."

Four hours later, even Olivia seemed exhausted, but she had not complained even once. Their hands had bloody blisters with splinters poking out of them. Their legs were bruised from the platforms banging against them with each step. Their arms were covered with scratches from tired missteps that led them too close to bramble bushes along the trail. They had stopped talking and appreciating their work after the second platform. After recovering from his fall, Bear had stopped thinking about giving up. He knew they could do it and he was conserving his energy. *Slow and steady* had guided every step. In the end they were their slowest and far from steady, stumbling over twigs on the trail, too tired to lift their feet off the ground. They shuffled sluggishly back to Olivia's house.

"There's a shortcut. It's kind of rough," were the only words spoken before Olivia veered into the brambles alongside the path.

Bear followed her toward a nearly dry stream bed, not caring about the mud grabbing at his shoes. He checked the scratches on his arms and pushed branches out of his way as they made their way back. Olivia let go of a long wild rose bough. It swung back and the thorns tore into Bear's face. Too tired to complain, he winced as he silently pulled each thorn from his cheek before struggling to catch up with Olivia.

At the sound of Victor's rich booming voice singing opera, Bear looked up and saw the back of the Anayas' blue house. He had gotten turned around again and was too tired to try and sort it out. They came around the side of the home and stopped to look at Victor waving his muscular arms, conducting an imaginary orchestra to the melody he was singing. Olivia and Bear grinned at each other before bumping fists. They had done it. They were ready to catch a poacher.

Bear looked toward Victor again and saw his grandmother, Honey, the Professor, Zoe the taxi driver, and then Mrs. Frost emerge from behind the brush that edged the Anayas' driveway on the far side of the yard. His eyes widened. What time was it? How had he forgotten that he was supposed to be home at lunchtime?

"We have company," Olivia said before running to greet the visitors.

Honey raced across the lawn, jumped up on Bear, and nearly knocked him over. He focused all of his attention on the dog, avoiding making eye contact with any of the adults who were slowly walking towards him. Bear got down on his knees to pet the dog and hide behind her.

"Oh, Honey, I'm in trouble now. How mad are they, girl?" he whispered.

When he finally had the courage to look toward his grandmother and her neighbors, he saw that they were huddled together, deep in conversation with Victor Anaya. No one was paying any attention to him. After a few more minutes he and Honey slowly approached the group in the middle of the yard.

Fragments of their conversation drifted to him: "I never said you look down on me for being in a wheelchair." Victor's booming voice was the easiest to hear. "But Bear said..." It was hard to hear his grandmother. "I felt terrible...we never..." And then the whole group turned to watch Bear and Honey's slow approach.

His grandmother broke from the group and strode toward him. "Berend Houtman, you scared us half to death. Don't you ever do to that to me again!" And then she wrapped her arms around him. "I was so worried. I didn't know where you were, or if something terrible had happened to you." She took a step back, held onto his hands and looked closely at him. "Your parents trust me. This isn't like you, Buckaroo Bear. What happened to your face?" His grandmother's eyes, the mirror image of her grandson's, widened as she touched his bloody cheek before examining the cut on his chin.

It was hard for Bear to meet her gaze. He knew she was right but he also knew she was wrong. "Gramma." he took a breath for courage. "You're the one that taught me— taught me to respect the environment." She dipped her head slightly. When she didn't speak, his confidence grew. "I wouldn't know what a lady's slipper or a beaver lodge was—or care—if it wasn't for you." He pulled his hands back from hers and stared down at them as he spoke, "This is important."

"We found more traps," Olivia blurted. Bear looked up and saw his friend standing beside him. "And someone took more lady's slippers."

"You must be very proud of your grandson," Victor said from the other side of his grandmother. "They've done more work today than most grownups could do in a week."

"Now you're just ganging up on me." Bear's grandmother smiled.

"So, you won't mind spending a night in a tree stand?" Victor asked. Everyone looked confused. "We have four platforms and only two kids."

"Cool," Zoe said. Bear had never heard her speak before and was startled to hear the silky voice that came from her outward sloppiness. "Count me in."

"What about me?" The Professor stepped forward.

Olivia and Bear looked at each other and mouthed, *wow!* They shook their heads in surprise.

Bear felt a light tap on his shoulder. When he looked over he saw Mrs. Frost beaming at him, one hand on her cane and the other in a fist extended toward him. The ninety-year-old woman and the eleven-year-old boy bumped fists and hollered "Kaboom!" to the surprise of everyone around them.

They hugged and she whispered in his ear, "Never wait for permission to follow your heart."

12

His grandmother and her neighbors had been concerned about Bear when they arrived at the Anayas'
house. But their concern was replaced with understanding and excitement as they heard about Bear and Olivia's
activities. Victor insisted that they stay and have something to eat.

"Let's celebrate what the kids accomplished today."

Starving after their long day working in the woods,
Bear and Olivia were overjoyed.

Victor sang as he washed the carrots and cherry toma-
toes Olivia had picked from their garden. At the sound of
the first note, Zoe dashed back to her taxi and returned
with a guitar to accompany him. Olivia zipped around
the kitchen, getting a jug of their homemade apple cider
and putting cheese and sliced meat on a platter for sand-

wiches. Bear settled into a kitchen chair. The sight of all the food made his stomach growl as he watched the activity around him. Olivia and Victor brought everyone up to date about the tree stands, traps, and damage to beaver dams.

Bear looked suspiciously at the rolls Olivia was slicing. There were green flecks all over them. Was Olivia too tired to see that they were moldy? Every muscle ached as he pushed himself up from the chair to whisper his concern. He didn't want to embarrass her in front of everyone.

"Those rolls are moldy. You have to throw them out."

"Are not. I baked them yesterday." She gave him a questioning look. "That's rosemary and sea salt."

Bear sat down. Now he was the one who was embarrassed. He wondered if it was possible to eat around the green spots.

Mrs. Frost had taken over the planning. "Oh, dear, let's see, you'll all need head lamps if you're going into the woods before sunrise. We don't want you to step in a trap." Olivia handed her a piece of paper and a pen. Mrs. Frost jotted something down before continuing, "Sunrise is at 6. You should be in your trees by 5:30." She giggled at that sentence. "If you all leave together from Sally's at 5:15, can you make it?" She didn't wait for an answer. "Zoe, can you bring Olivia to our street?" Mrs. Frost's mind moved so much faster than her body, it made Bear smile.

Zoe strummed her guitar and sang her answer: "Yes. She said yes and what a surprise. Yes. She said yes and then closed her eyes."

Before Bear could register his shock at her beautiful voice and the strangely worded response, Victor joined in. "Yes. She said yes and opened her arms. Yes, she opened her arms and said yes."

Clearly, he sang more than just opera. Bear was surprised: Victor's musical tastes included songs that Zoe knew. He never imagined that Victor and Zoe would have anything in common. Bear applauded with the others when they finished. Victor bent forward at the waist to bow and acknowledge the clapping as he rolled over to the table carrying the platter of colorful vegetables.

There were purple carrots and white carrots, orange peppers and cucumbers the size of zucchini. Bear was too hungry to be bothered by the odd colors and sizes of the vegetables. He would have preferred potato chips but that was not an option. He took a bite of a roll, winced and hoped for the best. "Hey, this is pretty good." He was surprised.

Olivia rolled her eyes and said, "Thanks."

As Bear ate and enjoyed the chatter at the picnic table, his energy returned and the pain from his injuries faded. His grandmother had not found any traps at the Ward and Duncan estates.

"But I did notice the pond is getting awfully close to the Calhouns' new croquet court."

The Professor had made posters for his lecture on coexisting with wildlife and scheduled it for Saturday at the Seafarers' Museum. The adults fussed over Bear's scratches and scrapes. An unfamiliar quiet warmth filled him. He was proud of what they all had accomplished in one day. When Olivia talked about their adventures, she didn't make fun of him for falling. Instead, she talked about how hard it had been for both of them. No one would call him a little boy today.

Bear did have one nagging concern that kept wriggling into his brain, disrupting his enjoyment of all they had accomplished. He was not sure that the Professor would be able to climb a tree. And they were counting on him. There was no denying that the Professor had a way with words. He spent most of his time with books. But tomorrow they would need him to be nimble and flexible. If he couldn't pull his giant body up a tree they had to find out today. But Bear knew better than to ask him about his recent tree-climbing experience.

"Hey, Zoe," Bear said, "can you drive the four of us to the backshore?" He gestured toward Zoe, Olivia, and the Professor. "If we sneak into the woods by the Ward estate, we can show you where the tree stands are. Gus said they've left for the season."

"Good idea," Olivia said and nodded approvingly at Bear. "They could be hard to find tomorrow morning in the dark."

Zoe parked the cherry red taxi on the ocean side of Atlantic Avenue before the four of them raced up the Duncans' driveway and disappeared behind the ornate stone garage. Once they reached the woods they relaxed, knowing they were out of sight of the Burneside and Calhoun properties.

As they walked through the woods, the Professor and Zoe remarked several times on how rough the trail was. When they saw the first platform they were in awe. They circled the tree. They said, "Victor is such a talented carpenter!" "Wow, you two got that up there?" At first Bear was flattered as he watched them walk around the tree repeating themselves. But after a few moments he became anxious. Were they stalling? Had either of them ever climbed a tree? When he looked at Olivia he saw the same concern on her face. The Professor and Zoe were still standing at the base of the tree. Neither one had made a move toward climbing it.

Zoe stopped moving. "It's so high," she said as she stared toward the treetops.

Bear turned to Olivia. "Let's show them."

With his back braced against the tree trunk, Bear laced his fingers together and cupped his hands in front of him.

Olivia put her right foot into his hands while reaching for the board they'd nailed to the tree above his head. Then she placed her left foot on Bear's shoulder as she reached for the second board nailed to the tree. Her third step was onto the bottom board on the tree before scrambling the rest of the way up the ladder and onto the tree stand. In less than a minute she was sitting on the platform grinning down at them.

Zoe looked impressed.

The Professor looked concerned. "Mr. Bear, how do you ascend the tree?"

Bear assumed the Professor was questioning his fitness and answered defensively. "The same way!"

The Professor shook his head and circled the tree one more time. "If Olivia is in a tree, how do you get onto another tree stand without her assistance?"

Olivia and Bear's eyes widened. They looked at each other before looking back at the Professor. But he was walking away from them, heading off the trail. Neither one acknowledged they had not thought of that. They had been so proud of themselves. The Professor returned, carrying a huge boulder. No one spoke as he dropped it at the base of the tree. Then he went back into the woods and came back with a thick broken branch shaped like a Y. He wedged it between the boulder and the tree trunk. He stepped on the boulder and then lifted his leg high to place his foot in the notch of the broken branch. His left hand reached for the second ladder board. His right hand grabbed the third and he pulled his right foot up to the bottom step. The board creaked and drooped beneath his weight. Unconcerned, he pushed away from the tree and gracefully dropped to the ground.

"Height has its advantages," he said as he brushed some tree bark from the front of his shirt. "It seemed unwise to join Olivia on the platform. I'm sure it wasn't designed for two." Olivia and Bear nodded.

Bear was impressed. He had no idea the Professor could solve a problem that wasn't in a textbook. Maybe he really was smart. He clearly wasn't as clumsy as Bear had assumed.

As Olivia came down from the tree she said, "This can be the Professor's tree. He has his steps here already." She gestured to the rock and tree limb. "Tomorrow morning we'll have to come in from the Wards' property, since the Professor is the only one who doesn't need help getting up." Everyone nodded. "We better keep moving if we're going to get out of the woods by dark."

Olivia and Bear jogged ahead to the next tree stand.

"Zoe you try this one," Bear said.

Bear braced his back against the tree but quickly realized Zoe weighed more than Olivia and he might not be able to support her. "Hey, Professor, can you boost her?"

The Professor stepped into position with his back against the tree. Olivia and Bear showed him how to link his hands and brace himself. Zoe placed her right hiking boot into the Professor's cupped hands. She tugged on his head as she struggled to place her left foot on his shoulder. The hem of her long flowing skirt snagged on her boot. Olivia reached to gather up the folds of the orange and purple flowery fabric and hold them to the side. As Zoe grasped the first ladder board just above the Professor's head she made a second attempt to step on his shoulder. Instead, her hiking boot crashed into his jaw. He hollered, reached for his face, and dropped Zoe's other foot. As she began to fall backwards, Olivia and Bear jumped forward to catch her. They all tumbled to the ground at the Professor's feet.

"Sorry," he said as he rubbed his jaw. "Awfully sorry. Is anyone injured?"

As Bear rolled out from underneath Zoe he mumbled, "You'd think a tree hugger could climb a tree."

"Tree hugger? I'm a singer, dude."

"You can be both," Olivia said. "You guys want to try that again? First, you better tuck that skirt into your jeans.

The second attempt was a success. Zoe sat in her tree grinning with her bright skirt billowing around her waist. "What a view! Hey there's a bird's nest right there." She pointed and then looked across the pond. "Dudes, it looks like someone's putting sand bags next to a croquet court. Totally bizarre."

"Calhouns," Bear and Olivia said together.

"Zoe," the Professor began, "your skirt…"

"What's wrong with my skirt?"

Bear tried to be diplomatic. "It's kinda…visible. And we're trying to be invisible…"

"You can't wear it. Just wear your jeans," Olivia said before she began jogging down the trail to the next tree.

Bear didn't wait for a response; he ran after Olivia. Behind him he could hear the adults talking as the Professor helped Zoe out of her tree. "I always wear a skirt. Do you really think it's a problem?"

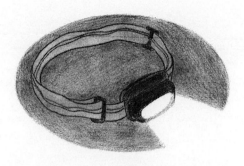

13

The next morning, Zoe and Olivia arrived at Sally Parker's home in the deep, early dark, excited to be so close to catching the elusive poacher before any more animals were hurt. Bear was relieved to see Zoe had left her bright floral skirt at home. Her clothing was gray and practical for moving through the woods. Olivia was wearing the same clothes she'd had on when Bear had met her.

After a big breakfast they grabbed their headlamps, met the Professor in the middle of Maple Street, and climbed into the taxi. The cherry red minivan cruised silently around the island, headlights turned off as the waves crashed against the rocks beside the road. Last night, lying in bed and imagining this moment, Bear had been excited and eager. Now it was scary. He began chewing on a fingernail and willed Zoe to drive faster. They had to be in their trees before the poacher entered the woods. Olivia gently punched him on the shoulder and gave him the thumbs-up signal.

The taxi coasted into the Wards' driveway and came to a stop behind the hedges. No one spoke as they exited the van with their headlamps clutched in their hands. Quietly, quickly they moved across the lawn toward the pond, then around its edge and into the woods. For the first time they paused and turned on their headlamps. With silent nods and determined smiles they moved forward. Even with their headlamps it was hard to see the roots and rocks that could trip them. Every step seemed to echo through the gloomy woods. No one spoke. The Professor silently boosted Bear into his tree before the others quickly moved down the path to Olivia's tree.

Bear switched off his headlamp and wiggled, struggling to find a position he could comfortably hold for the next hour. He was struck by the silent stillness around him. He was completely alone. It was as if the dark woods had swallowed the Professor, Zoe, and Olivia. The flickering light of their headlamps had vanished. He strained but couldn't hear their footfalls. The only sound was the creaking of tree branches bending in the breeze. He wished Honey were by his side. The thought of the golden retriever climbing a tree made him smile as he leaned back against the tree trunk and closed his eyes.

He must have dozed. When he opened his eyes a narrow strip of sky was beginning to glow orange, low on the horizon, behind the trees. He leaned forward to stare toward the trail's beginning. A shape moved cautiously toward him. Bear shook his head, closed his eyes, and looked again. It was still there, definitely a person, moving slowly in the half light.

As the figure moved closer, the crows began to stir, responding to the movement on the trail. Their caws grew louder with each step. It must be a man, Bear thought, but a small man. Maybe he looks small because I'm so high. Bear strained to see who it was, but the stranger was wearing a baggy dark sweatshirt with the hood pulled up. The person raised his hands to cover his head in response to the crows. Was he afraid they were going to swoop down and peck him? If this was their poacher, he wasn't a woodsman. The stranger looked more anxious than Bear had ever felt, even as a little boy, in the woods.

The dark figure was almost beneath Bear. What should he do? They hadn't planned this part. Was he supposed to jump on the suspect? It was a long way down to the ground. Besides, Bear had learned to keep his hands to himself and not make false accusations. He had to know for sure that this was the lawless trapper before he risked injuring anyone, including himself.

Bear twisted, trying to get a better view. A board squeaked. He pulled back. Slowly he leaned over the platform's edge, trying to see the poacher's face. Bear needed a description. The hood of the sweatshirt was low on the stranger's forehead and he was hunched over. It could be anyone. From Bear's position it was impossible to even guess his height. All Bear could see were the man's hands. If the shuffling figure was a man. Maybe Olivia would have a better view.

There was rustling further down the path, followed by a loud thud. Bear grabbed the tree trunk to steady himself. What was that? Even the crows were shocked into silence. The quiet was broken by the sound of footsteps running. It was the hooded man, running, stumbling, tripping, careening down the path. Was someone chasing him? Had Olivia tried to jump on him? Bear could hear his heart pounding. He leaned over the edge, afraid of what he would see. The hooded person stumbled back to his feet before running out of the woods. Bear collapsed against the tree trunk, clutched his hands to his chest, and felt the thud of his heart. It seemed like he sat that way for days before he heard a twig snap behind him.

"Hey," Olivia whispered, "what happened?"

Bear shrugged his shoulders and raised his hands to gesture that he didn't know. Olivia waved for him to come down. Slowly, quietly, they made their way down the trail to the tree where Zoe perched. When they got there, her head was sticking out over the side of the platform, dreadlocks swaying in the breeze, her eyes the size of ping pong balls.

"Dudes, what was that noise?" Her usually smooth voice sounded shrill with fear.

"Shh!" Bear and Olivia each held a finger to their lips.

But she kept talking. "I'm getting some bad vibes. Get me outa this tree."

"Shh!"

"Was that him? He didn't make it all the way to my tree, but I saw someone coming."

"Quiet!" Olivia said loudly before gesturing for Zoe to come down.

Bear and Olivia shook their heads at Zoe's lack of detective skills. They braced their backs against the tree so she could step onto their shoulders before dropping down to the ground. The three of them followed the trail to the Professor's tree stand. With each step forward Bear expected to see the Professor walking toward them. With each step and no sign of the Professor, Bear was more concerned.

Bear tugged on Olivia's sleeve and whispered, "He should've met us by now."

Then they saw him. The Professor lay face down on the trail with the tree platform on the back of his legs. Bear froze, staggered, and stared. The Professor wasn't moving. Bear raced to his friend's side and looked back toward Olivia and Zoe. He looked for guidance and saw shock.

The crows resumed their loud cawing.

"Run to the taxi," Olivia screamed at Zoe. "Drive to the police station. They'll call the fireboat and send the island ambulance and EMT here. You'll have to show them the way. They'll never find us out here."

Olivia turned to Bear and the Professor. "Don't move him. Whatever you do, don't move him." She walked slowly toward Bear as tears rolled down her cheeks. "Is he alive?"

Bear nodded. He could see the Professor's back rising and falling. Bear was almost as alarmed by Olivia's crying as he was by the sight of the silent professor.

Olivia pushed Bear aside and knelt beside the Professor. "It's just like my dad," she said and wiped her tears with the back of her hand. "Just like Dad. You can't move him." Her voice was quiet. Was she talking to herself? "Don't move him. Don't move him."

Bear carefully removed the platform from the Professor's legs then picked up his glasses. Bear wiped them off before placing them in his coat pocket. He stepped back to watch his two friends. Bear yearned to be helpful, but he had never felt more helpless.

"It's just like Dad." Her body shivered. She took the Professor's hand in both of hers. "Professor, can you hear me?" Bear leaned toward them, hoping for a response. There was none. "Professor, it's Olivia. Everything's going to be okay," she snuffled. "Bear's here too. We're just waiting…" The Professor's eyelids fluttered. Bear fell to his knees beside Olivia.

They stared and hoped that he would lecture them. Instead, he moaned. Before Olivia could stop the Professor, he rolled onto his back. His face contorted with a grimace. Olivia and Bear gasped at the sight of his bloody face.

"My leg," the Professor groaned. "What's wrong with my leg?"

Olivia and Bear looked and saw his left leg jutting off at an unnatural angle. Bear felt sick. He had never seen anything so horrible in his whole life.

But Olivia's voice steadied, "You're going to be okay." She smiled as the tears slid down her face. "You're going to be okay."

The sun was above the horizon when they finally heard Zoe pounding down the trail, running toward them.

"Here they come," Olivia and Bear said in unison.

Olivia leaned in to whisper, "They're coming, Professor. Everything's going to be okay." His head bobbed once with acknowledgment.

"Paramedics are right behind me." Zoe was breathless but still managed to shout. "We've got the ambulance and the taxi at the Duncan estate. That's the closest we could get." She came to a stop and put her hands on her hips as she gasped for breath. "Mrs. Frost is waiting in the taxi."

"What?" Olivia and Bear spoke over each other.

Bear left the Professor's side to ask Zoe. "Why'd you bring Mrs. Frost?" He didn't want his frail, elderly friend to see the Professor like this.

Zoe grabbed his arm and pulled Bear out of the way as the paramedics pushed past them to attend to the Professor. "Dude, someone has to go to the hospital with Malcolm. I'd do it, but I'm supposed to drive the taxi all day and your grandmother has her hands full with you."

"Hey!" He yanked his arm from her grasp, offended by her comment.

"Dude!"

He knew she was right. "Yeah." He took three steps toward the paramedics before stopping and turning back to Zoe. "Thanks…for thinking of that." The words came out more easily than he had expected.

"No worries. I've got you covered."

14

Within minutes of the paramedics beginning to work on the Professor, Bear sensed they were concerned about something. Their eyes darted around as they put a splint on the Professor's left leg. Bear heard fragments of their conversation: "trails too rough," "can't drive closer," "those three? Nah."

"Malcolm," one of them said, "you're a big guy. Did you play pro ball?"

"He's a professor, not an athlete," Bear said.

"You can be both," Olivia and Zoe said together.

"Well, Professor Malcolm," the EMT continued, "you're tall enough to play for the Boston Celtics. We need to get you out of here as smoothly as possible." He examined Zoe, Olivia, and Bear but seemed unimpressed. He looked at the other EMT and shook his head.

Bear started chewing on his thumb nail. They could drag him out on the tree platform, but every bump on the trail would increase the Professor's pain. Olivia was stripping the bark off a tree branch as Zoe tugged on her dreadlocks. It didn't look like either one of them had a solution.

"We can help. We have to. Come on . . ." Bear pleaded. But the look in everyone's eyes silenced him. If they tried to carry the Professor and dropped him it would be excruciating.

As Bear's hopes faded, his grandmother appeared on the trail. Behind her were Gus and Mike Mooney.

"Gus showed up with the newspaper." His grandmother began talking as soon as she saw them. "I told him the situation and we realized you might need some help."

"So, they called me," Mike Mooney joked. "I'm the muscles of the operation." He knelt beside the Professor. "How're you doing?"

"Better," he mouthed.

"Let's get this show on the road," Mike Mooney said. "Where do you want us?" It was hard to watch: The Professor's face pulled taut with pain and his hands balled into tight fists. Not one sound escaped his clenched jaws as they moved his large frame onto the stretcher. Bear turned away, afraid he would scream. When he looked back, Zoe and the men were slowly carrying the stretcher down the uneven trail, followed by Bear's grandmother. They struggled to avoid the rocks and roots, holding the stretcher as steady as possible.

Olivia and Bear sank onto a log. They sat in silence. After several minutes, Bear picked up a stick and began to doodle in the dirt.

"He's going to be okay." Olivia looked at Bear's doubtful face and continued, "As soon as he's in the ambulance they'll give him something for the pain. When he's on the fire boat, as it's heading to Portland, they'll stitch up his forehead and get that bandaged. Another ambulance will meet the boat in Portland and drive him to the hospital." Bear didn't look convinced. Olivia tried again. "I bet he's in a hospital room relaxing and watching TV before we get home."

"The Professor hates TV."

Olivia sighed. "We need to clean this up," she gestured at the broken tree stand, "just in case the poacher comes back. We don't want to give anything away."

"Yeah." Bear looked up for the first time. "Do you think we should try again?"

Olivia nodded.

"Then we have to rebuild the tree stand."

Olivia shook her head. "Three are enough."

"I could ask my grandmother. I know she'd do it. She can climb a tree. I've seen her."

"No." Olivia looked directly at him. "She'd do it but it'd be wrong to ask."

Bear knew she was right.

"Your grandmother's more important than any plant or beaver. I know she's a lot smaller than the Professor, but I can't stand the thought of anyone else climbing this tree." Olivia looked at the boards they had nailed to the tree trunk and shook her head. "Let's clean up this mess. We can hide it in the brush over there. We'll come back and get it later."

When they returned to his grandmother's cottage, the aroma of the morning's hearty breakfast of biscuits, bacon, and eggs, was gone. Their eager mood and animated breakfast conversation were forgotten. It had all been replaced by dread. Sooner or later Mrs. Frost would call. The phone would ring. How bad would the news be? Bear and Olivia each sat on a couch. They faced each other but didn't make eye contact. Olivia wove her fingers together: over, under, over, under, and then started again. Bear picked little bits of bark, pine needles, and leaves off his clothing before deliberately arranging a tiny pile of woods' litter on his left leg.

"Hey, kiddoes," his grandmother called from the kitchen, "do you want to bake cookies or something?"

"Nah."

"No," Olivia said. "Thanks, though."

"She'll call when she knows something. Sitting here won't make her call any sooner."

Bear swept the leaf and bark bits into his hand. "Want to help me stack his wood?" he asked Olivia.

She responded by jumping up and walking to the door. Bear was right behind her.

Standing in front of the wood that had been dumped in Malcolm Yeats's yard, Olivia said, "Some folks, like my dad, are fussy about how they stack. What about the Professor?"

Bear began to explain how the end pieces had to be big, with one flat side so they would be strong and stable. He scanned the split pieces of hard wood, searching for an example of sturdy pieces for the supporting edges, pieces that would keep the long row of wood upright for months to come. Each species had a different grain and coloring. Bear got an idea. "What if we make a picture?" He picked up a piece of oak and looked at the yellow in its grain before grabbing a pink-toned piece of red maple. He set them side by side and then put a piece of white paper birch beside them. "With the maple and oak we can have the cut ends facing out and with the birch we have the white bark showing."

"We could make seagulls flying in the wood pile," Olivia said as she arranged some birch wood on the ground, two white arches joined to look like a bird in flight.

"Yeah, or waves in the ocean." Bear squatted next to her, quickly arranging the wood in the shape of crashing surf.

"Or a lighthouse?"

"Yeah!" Bear started to smile and then thought about the Professor. "It might cheer him up. It can be our apology too." A piece of firewood dangled from each hand as he stared at the ground. "I was afraid that platform wasn't strong enough. I should've said something."

Olivia nodded. "We owe him. That's for sure."

Building on top of what had been stacked days earlier, Bear created an island of horizontal split-oak firewood. With the bark facing outward, the wood resembled the rocky coast of Maine. On top of his island, he began a white lighthouse of paper birch. Beside him Olivia created an ocean of round oak end cuts. She topped this with curving paper birch waves under a red maple sunset sky.

They were so intent on their work that they didn't notice the taxi pulling up in front of Mrs. Frost's cottage until Zoe hollered at them, "Totally awesome, dudes!" She was helping Victor get out of the taxi and into his wheelchair.

Olivia ran over to hug her father. "Did Zoe tell you? I'm sorry I didn't come home. I didn't know what to say."

"It's okay." Victor held Olivia's hands and looked into her face. "It's okay. Zoe said it shouldn't be anything worse than a broken leg."

"What're you doing?" Bear asked as he watched Zoe pulling lumber out of the back of the taxi. She stacked it next to two saw-horses.

"Wasn't I supposed to tell him?" Zoe looked back and forth between Olivia and her father. "I didn't know. I totally figured he'd want to know."

Victor reached out to touch Zoe's arm. "It's all right. I'm glad you told me. I was starting to worry about this one." He gestured toward Olivia. "I wondered why she hadn't come home or called."

"Sorry, Dad."

"I understand."

Bear was becoming impatient. "What's the lumber for?"

"Hey there," his grandmother called from her porch. "I'm glad you're here," she said when she saw Zoe and Victor. "Viola just called. He's out of surgery. They have the leg in a cast so he can't bend it at the knee." She looked down at a piece of paper in her hand. "He'll be in a wheelchair for at least a month."

"We figured," Zoe and Victor said together.

"He has a concussion too, and some stitches in his face. They'll keep him in the hospital overnight for observation. She's going to stay there with him." Bear's grandmother looked out at everyone and smiled. "I'd say that's all pretty good news. Oh, and the Professor doesn't know it yet, but he's going to be staying at Viola's until he's out of the wheelchair."

"That's what the wood's for," Victor said to Bear, finally answering his question. "He's going to need a wheelchair ramp."

"How'd you know?"

"Experience," Victor tapped his hands on his wheel-chair's armrests. Bear was embarrassed by his stupid question. "Honestly, I'm excited. If all of you had wheelchair ramps, I could visit."

Maple Street had never been so busy. Olivia and Bear continued stacking wood, putting the finishing touches on their wooden mural of coastal Maine at sunset. On the other side of the street, Victor, Zoe, and Sally Parker began building a wheelchair ramp at Mrs. Frost's. Victor sang an aria as he used his circular saw. Sally and Zoe tried to hammer to the beat of his melody and laughed at their failure.

Bear thought about what Victor had said about the wheelchair ramp. It was great that his home was accessible, but it would be even better if his friends' homes were too. Bear couldn't imagine not being able to go and visit a friend. Stacking wood, looking for the right piece, placing it, stepping back to see the tower of the lighthouse emerge, he remembered what the Professor had said two days before: "My analytical faculties are always strengthened by manual labor." Bear hadn't understood him at the time, but it was starting to make sense as his hands worked and his mind wandered.

"I had a thought," Olivia said quietly. "I know we promised my dad we wouldn't dump red paint on the guy, but we have to do something."

Bear instantly understood. He recalled the moment when he had been sitting in the tree stand, watching the person stumbling through the woods toward him with his dark sweatshirt and hood concealing his face. "I didn't know what to do—jump on him, climb down and chase him? I couldn't tell you what he looked like other than that he didn't seem very big and he has hands. That's not very helpful. What if it was just someone going for a walk in the woods?"

"Right!" Olivia glanced at the adults working across the street. She moved closer to Bear and whispered, "We have to mark the suspect so he can be identified later, but we have to do it in a way that doesn't harm him, in case we're wrong."

"How do we do that?"

"Sumac berries, skunk cabbage, and super soakers."

Bear's jaw dropped. "Huh?"

Olivia held a finger up to her lips and jerked her head toward the adults on the other side of Maple Street. "We'll finish up, then make an excuse to leave," she whispered. "We have to do this while Dad's busy here." The sound of his singing floated across the dirt road and they returned to stacking wood with newfound energy.

Bear and Olivia finished working on the white paper birch seagulls. They stepped back to admire their work: on the left, a white lighthouse perched on a small island pointed toward the sky. Wooden birch waves rose from the ocean and crashed against the island. In the sky, three seagulls flew through the wooden pink sunset.

"Stacking wood art." Victor was beside them. His rapid silent movements still surprised Bear. "I'm impressed."

"You two," Zoe said as she crossed the road to join them, "aren't like regular kids."

Bear stared at Zoe, ready to take offense.

"You two are something special." Zoe shook her head, a look of amazement on her face. "Totally cool!"

"He's going to love it. It's beautiful." Bear's grandmother put one arm around him and the other around Olivia and gave them both a squeeze. "You deserve a break. Can I give you money for ice cream?"

Just like that they were able to get away and start work on their plan. Bear was relieved he didn't have to come up with an explanation for his grandmother. He shoved the money in his pocket and ran to catch up with Olivia.

15

Bear and Olivia ran down Wharf Street toward the Goofy Gull Gift Shop. Bear had been on the island for five whole days and hadn't been in the gift shop yet. That had to be a record. Nothing about this trip to Oxbow Island was like any of his previous visits to his grandmother's.

"How much did she give you?" Olivia asked.

"Twenty."

"I've got some money too. The store is having their end of summer sale. Should be enough." Olivia slowed to walk as they reached Water Street. "Hope they still have the giant squirt guns."

Bear grabbed her arm and pulled her back from the street.

"What's wrong with you?" Her annoyance was obvious.

"Turn around," Bear hissed. "It's Floyd Flood."

153

Olivia shrugged. "So?"

"The animal control officer," Bear said.

Floyd Flood was hunched over as he walked down the sidewalk. His head swiveled and his eyes glared.

"Maybe he could help us," Olivia said. "He must walk the island every day, talk to a lot of people, know what's going on…"

"No," Bear interrupted. "Even Honey hates him. He's horrible. He wrote her a ticket. Said she charged at him. She just ran to him with her tail wagging, like she always does."

When the animal control officer was out of sight, they raced across Water Street to the Goofy Gull Gift Shop. Again, Bear grabbed Olivia by the arm and tugged her.

"What is wrong with you?" Olivia looked almost as angry as the first time he met her. "Do not grab me."

Bear raised his index finger to his lips before pointing down Wharf Street to the line of cars waiting for the next ferry

The Calhouns and Burnesides were standing on the sidewalk beside two sparkling cars.

"Do you think they're leaving?" Olivia asked.

"They're in line for the next car ferry."

The blonde Mrs. Burneside reached into the car beside her and removed something. Oblivious to the people walking past, she carefully applied lipstick and checked her hand mirror before making a slight correction at the corner of her lips.

Olivia turned to Bear and did a perfect imitation. Laughing, they stepped into the Goofy Gull. Bear paused but Olivia knew exactly where to go. Past the coffee mugs with pictures of lighthouses, she turned down an aisle that overflowed with stacks of sweatshirts and T-shirts. On the far wall, beneath the Christmas ornaments decorated with sailboats, were the toys.

"They're still here!" Olivia aimed a sky-blue Super Soaker Squirt Gun at him and grinned. It was as big as a backpack. "There's one for you too. And," she pointed at the giant banner above the ornaments, "everything's 75 percent off. End of season sale."

Bear grabbed a squirt gun and followed her to the register. They walked past the ice cream counter without even checking to see what flavors remained after Labor Day. There wasn't time or money for ice cream today.

"We have to hurry. We need to gather the sumac and skunk cabbage in the woods and prepare it before Dad finishes that ramp and gets home."

As they pushed open the gift shop's door Bear saw his grandmother walking down Wharf Street with Honey the Wonder Dog. She was heading straight for them.

"Hide, it's Gramma!"

With their squirt guns clutched to their chests they scurried behind the racks of postcards until his grandmother and Honey were out of sight. "Hope they don't run into Floyd Flood," Bear said as he looked down the street. "Gramma could get in a fight with him."

Side by side, Olivia and Bear trotted down the street. The squirt guns, attached to shoulder straps, bounced lightly against their backs, echoing the rhythm of their feet. A plan evolved with each step toward the woods: Olivia would gather the sumac flowers, Bear would pick the skunk cabbage leaves, and then they would meet back at Olivia's house to prepare the stinky dye for their squirt guns. Bear smiled when he realized he wasn't struggling to keep up with Olivia. He could run and talk without gasping for breath.

Olivia spotted the maroon spikes of sumac flowers topping the branches of a small tree beside the marsh. She turned onto a narrow path. The tall marsh grass quickly hid her from view.

"Watch out for traps," Bear hollered and continued into the woods.

There was a large patch of skunk cabbage on the South Loop Trail near the saltwater marsh. As he tore off the first leaf, an unmistakable rancid odor was released. He dropped the leaf and stepped back. With a gulp, he filled his lungs with fresh air, held his breath, and charged at the low growing plants. His left hand held out the bottom of his T-shirt while his right hand grabbed clumps of leaves and shoved them into his shirt pouch. When he was desperate for air, he rolled the bottom of his shirt around the leaves and jumped back. His feet could not carry him fast enough away from the stench beside the bridge. As he ran, he realized the foul odor was coming with him, wrapped in his shirt, clutched against his belly.

When Bear arrived at Olivia's, she was bringing an extension cord to the picnic table. Before he could get her attention, she walked back to the house and returned with a food processor.

"What're you doing?" he asked.

"I smelled you before I saw you," she said. "You'll work out here. By the time you're done it'll be even stinkier. Too smelly to mix inside." She returned to the house for cider vinegar and then dug up horseradish root, the size of a baseball, from the garden.

Bear watched her, listened to her directions, and concluded that she was over-reacting. The skunk cabbage was bad but the scent seemed to have faded. If that were the case how would it ever help them catch their suspect? Maybe it hadn't faded and he had just gotten used to it. Bear lifted a leaf to his nose. He immediately dropped it back on the table. It still reeked.

"Don't eat that. It could kill you," Olivia said as she returned to the house. "I'm boiling the sumac for the dye. I'll bring it out when I'm done. Do not come in the house." She pulled the door shut behind her.

Bear began to tear up the leaves and drop them into the food processor. With each rip the smell became worse. Why would anyone eat this? Trying to block the smell, he pulled his T-shirt up over his nose and mouth, gagged, and remembered that's where he'd carried the leaves. He backed up from the picnic table. He had to do this quickly or he would vomit. He threw all the leaves into the food processor, poured in half the bottle of cider vinegar, tossed in the horseradish root, and then stepped away for another breath. The smell of vinegar was surprisingly pleasant. He was sure the worst was behind him. He returned to the picnic table, put the lid on the food processor, and pushed the power button.

The machine whirred and the mixture erupted through an opening on the lid he had forgotten to cap. The liquid splattered the front of his shirt. He heard the machine grinding up the horseradish and skunk cabbage leaves as the cold liquid soaked through his shirt. Suddenly his other senses were assaulted. The inside of his nose was on fire, his eyes watered and the back of his throat tightened. Bear stumbled backwards as the machine continued chopping and blending the ingredients. He gasped for fresh air. He wiped the tears from his eyes with the back of his hand and immediately regretted it. It must be the horseradish root. The ingredients had been smelly but tolerable until the root was sliced open by the food processer's blades

Olivia opened the door. Was she laughing at him? She took one whiff, waved him away and closed the door. She returned with a large glass of water but she made him move far away before she opened the door and placed it on the ground. Was the water for him or the stink bomb? He took a sip and poured the rest into the whirring food processor. More of the nauseating mix splashed on his shirt. Enough. He shut off the food processor and retreated to the vegetable garden to wait for Olivia. He pulled up a purple carrot, wiped the dirt off on his pants, and began to eat it. Was the stink fading or had he lost all sense of smell and taste? Bear wasn't sure.

Olivia appeared at the door with a large pot. "We have to mix the stink with the dye." Bear approached to help her but she cringed. "You smell really bad."

"I'll do it," Bear said as he took the pot from her. "No point in both of us stinking."

Olivia spoke through a small opening in the door. "Dump the skunk cabbage mix in the dye, then load it in the squirt guns." She stepped away from the door before reappearing with a funnel, baggies, and rubber bands that she dropped outside the door. "Use the funnel so it doesn't get all over the outside of the guns or we'll both stink. Too late for you," she said with a laugh. "Use the rubber bands to hold the baggies on the end of each squirt gun so it doesn't drip all over us tomorrow."

"I'm starting to like the smell," Bear joked.

When Bear had finished he gave Olivia a thumbs up and she came out of the house.

"I can smell you all the way over here. You can't go home like that." She plugged her nose. "Want to jump off the dock? That'll knock the stink off of you."

Every summer kids on Oxbow Island gathered at the dock to jump into the cold Atlantic Ocean. Then they climbed fifteen feet up the metal ladder, back to the dock. Bear liked hearing their shrieks and watching the brave ones climbing even higher, to jump from the tops of pilings. Some did flips. Others leapt in big groups holding hands and screaming the whole time they were in the air. Bear had never jumped. When he was nine, he said he would do it when he was ten and when he was ten, he said he would do it when he was eleven. Another summer had passed and he hadn't joined the dock-jumping kids. He had felt relief at avoiding it for one more year.

"I don't know." Bear squirmed and tugged at his wet, smelly T-shirt.

"It's either that or I have to hose you off."

Somehow that seemed worse. So, they hid the squirt guns by the vegetable garden and ran toward the dock.

For the first time since he had met Olivia Anaya, she ran behind him, far behind him. When he looked back at her, she was still holding her nose.

Bear was pleased to see that no one else was at the dock and it was high tide. The water was a long way down, but he knew it would have been ten feet farther from him at low tide. He paced back and forth as Olivia scrambled to pull off her muddy boots.

"Aren't you going to take your shoes off?" she asked.

"I've never done this before," he admitted, staring at the ground and waiting for her to make fun of him. Kids almost half his age jumped every summer.

Olivia didn't laugh. She was matter of fact. "It's cold. That's for sure. But you'll be in the water for less than a minute." She looked at him. "Unless you want to swim around."

Bear shook his head.

"It's best to go in like a pencil, straight up and down. Figure out where the closest ladder is before you jump." Olivia pointed toward the water. "See, that's where you'll climb out." When Bear didn't move to look over the edge, Olivia lowered her voice, "Your fear is worse than the jump."

Bear glanced at her and realized she was right. He sat on the dock and untied his shoes, removed his socks, and carefully placed one sock in each shoe. Then he walked past her at a steady rate. His eyes were fixed on the city across the bay as he stepped off the dock.

Slipping through the air he was energized. The world was brighter, sparkling, as the crisp September air flowed past him. He was a super hero slicing through the sky. And then the water clutched his feet with a cold salty embrace. He was pulled under. Just as suddenly he was tossed back to the surface.

With his head thrown back, Bear yelled, "I jumped!" In that moment, Olivia leapt off the dock, flying over his head.

He had imagined that after landing in the ocean he would race to the ladder, eager to escape the icy water. Instead he treaded water, waiting for her to surface. "I did it!" he hollered when she popped up.

"Yup!" Her grin and high five said it all.

Bear did want to swim around. He wanted to hold on to this feeling that he could do anything. He wanted to see the ocean, city, island, sky from every angle. But when he turned back to the dock he saw Olivia pulling herself up the ladder. The clothes she had worn every day since Bear met her dripped streams of water.

"Are you coming?" she hollered over her shoulder.

Reluctantly, Bear swam to the dock and pulled himself out of the water. "Can you smell me now?" he said and laughed. "Can you smell me now?"

Olivia twitched and wrinkled her nose. "You smell like seaweed, and that's a big improvement."

They walked slowly up Wharf Street, Bear's face fixed in a grin. At the corner of Wharf and Water streets they ran into his grandmother. She was too preoccupied to notice that Bear and Olivia were soaking wet.

"The Calhouns and Burnesides left!" Olivia and Bear blurted.

"I know. I saw their cars in line for the ferry, so I went to their properties," she said. "I found a trap and a damaged beaver lodge between the Calhouns' and Burnesides' and a dozen dead lady's slippers in the garden. All at the Calhouns' estate.

"They left the island but there are still traps out there. Who's checking them?" Olivia asked. "Are they so terrible they would set traps and never check them for injured animals?"

Bear thought they might be.

16

Zoe, Olivia, and Bear ate breakfast in silence. The previous afternoon's accomplishments were forgotten. The Professor's horrible accident haunted them as they prepared to head back into the woods. Staring at his cereal, Bear was consumed by the image of the Professor's leg snapped in two.

"Maybe you shouldn't go." His grandmother opened and closed the lid on the cereal box. "You don't have to go. We know it's someone connected to the Calhoun estate. We can catch him there."

"Yeah," Bear said quietly. His grandmother was right but he wanted more evidence. He wanted to catch the poacher in the woods, with a trap, breaking the law. The only way to do that was to hide in the woods where the traps were.

Olivia stared directly at Bear, shaking her head *no* as Zoe looked back and forth between the two kids.

Slowly, Zoe stood. "Come on, dudes."

"I don't know. I don't like this." His grandmother stood between them and the door. She stared intently at the three young people.

Bear rose. "We got this," he said to himself.

"Okay. But if you aren't back here by six thirty, I'm coming looking for you." She stepped out of their way and lightly touched each of them as they walked past as if counting them.

Moving as a reluctant team, they headed out into the pre-dawn dark and climbed into the taxi. Bear stumbled over a bulky object behind the driver's seat.

"What's this?" Bear asked.

"My ladder."

Olivia and Bear looked confused.

"I can't get in the tree without the Professor. Remember? He gave me a boost. So, I made a macramé ladder," she said as she drove towards the backshore.

"Macramé?" Olivia and Bear said.

"I tied knots to make rungs between two pieces of rope. I think I can throw it up to the first board on the tree and pull myself up."

Bear was impressed. He had practiced different nautical knots but he'd never heard of macramé or making something with knots.

"What's with the guns?" Zoe asked as she tapped the squirt guns on Olivia's lap. "I figured you two were chill."

"They're not real," Bear began to explain, before realizing even Zoe wouldn't mistake their bright blue plastic squirt guns for real weapons.

"We filled them with a natural red dye, sumac. To help us track him down later." Olivia spoke casually and said nothing of the stench they had packed into each gun.

"Cool."

Bear nodded. They would know soon enough if it was cool or not.

There were no stumbles or hesitations as their head lamps guided them down the familiar trail. This time they knew what they were doing.

Bear sat in his tree stand with his head lamp shut off and felt his legs twitching uncontrollably. He clutched his thighs to his chest, but then the shaking spread through his whole body. With his head buried in his knees, he tried to wipe away the image of the Professor lying on the ground, pebbles and pinecones stuck in his bloody face.

A crow cawed and Bear's head snapped up in response. All his senses came alive. Something rustled far behind him. Probably alder leaves fluttering in the breeze. The sky had begun to shift from black to gray as the sun approached the horizon. Bear leaned forward, straining to see movement on the trail in front of him. There were only the dark silhouettes of trees edging the trail.

An unmistakable rancid odor filled his nose. He sat upright, his back braced against the tree trunk and fumbled for his squirt gun. The odor strengthened, but the trail in front of him was empty and he didn't hear movement behind him. Was it possible the poacher didn't know he had been stink-bombed? Had Olivia shot but missed him? Still, she would have gotten out of her tree after she emptied her gun. Bear waited, confused by the silence around him. He gripped his squirt gun, ready to shoot.

A light flickered below him and he shuddered. There were footsteps behind him. Steadily the light bounced up and down on the trail and trees. This morning the poacher had accessed the trail from the other end of the pond and he had a head lamp or flashlight. Yesterday must have scared him as much as it scared us, Bear thought. And then he heard it, the unmistakable gagging noise. The same sound Bear had made when he mixed Olivia's horseradish skunk recipe. The steps sped up, clumsy stumbling footfalls charging from behind his tree. Closer, closer. He must be trying to outrun the stink. Was Olivia chasing him? Bear leaned forward, his squirt gun hanging over the edge of his tree stand, waiting for the first sight of the poacher.

He appeared beneath Bear's tree stand, careening down the path. Dressed in the same dark sweatsuit, the poacher clutched a flashlight in one hand. Bear fired until his super soaker squirt gun was empty. The man was drenched in a smell he could not outrun. Lifting his hands to his head he stumbled away from Bear, off the trail, and away from the pond. Running blindly he crashed through the underbrush, heading up the hill toward the area that had been damaged in the Patriots' Day Storm.

Bear wiggled off his platform. When his feet were on the bottom ladder rung he pushed back from the tree and dropped down. Focused on catching the crook, he had forgotten to listen for the footfalls of Zoe and Olivia running down the trail, equally intent on catching the poacher. They collided with Bear before his feet even touched the ground. The impact threw him backwards. He landed on his back, the air knocked out of him. Olivia and Zoe tripped over each other and fell at his feet. By the time they were upright and brushing themselves off, the poacher was out of sight.

"He dropped a burlap bag when we started running after him." Olivia's jeans were torn from her fall. Her bloody knee was visible through the hole. "There's something in it."

"Dudes, what stinks?" Zoe asked as she examined her bloody elbow.

Bear had his own cuts and scrapes, but there was no time to check them. "Come on, we gotta stake out the Calhouns."

As they rushed to where the taxi was hidden at the Ward estate they made a plan. Zoe would pick up Victor and Sally Parker and bring them to the Calhoun estate. They were going to need everyone's help. Zoe raced away, screeching the taxi's tires as she pulled onto Atlantic Avenue.

Olivia and Bear jogged to the Calhouns' and raced to the back of the property, where they found a large patio with a swimming pool overlooking the croquet court. The poacher might come out of the woods at either end of the pond. With their noses, eyes, and ears attuned to their surroundings, they hurried and hid behind a massive stone barbecue grill. Kneeling, with only their heads visible, they were able to spy on the two possible access points. But if the poacher returned to the property from another direction, they would miss him. They needed Sally Parker, Zoe, and Victor on the lookout too. They wiggled, tried to get comfortable, and looked around, hoping to see their friends.

A tap on their shoulders made them jump.

"Shh!" Bear's grandmother held a finger to her lips as she squatted beside them. "Here are binoculars. Honey and I will cover the front of the house. Zoe and Victor are over there."

Bear grinned with relief. He leaned back and saw Victor and Zoe give a small wave from their spot behind the guest cottage. His grandmother and Honey slipped behind the shrubs next to the house. Everyone was in position. There was nothing left to do but wait. Olivia stared past the croquet court. Bear's head swiveled side to side between the two paths that exited the woods on each end of the pond. They passed the binoculars back and forth.

Bear's mind wandered. The poacher could be fleeing the island after what had happened in the woods. Nah, Bear thought. No one would board the ferry smelling the way the poacher did. Even if he rode outside, everyone would notice, stare, hold their noses, and talk about him. He was stuck on the island until he cleaned up and changed his clothes. Maybe he went somewhere else to clean up first and get rid of his smelly outfit.

Olivia jabbed Bear with her elbow. "Look!" She pointed toward the edge of the pond. A dark figure had waded into the murky water and grass at its edge. His knees jerked up and down, splashing the shallow, muddy water.

"Leeches?" Bear chuckled at the sight.

"Or snapping turtles," Olivia said with equal delight.

"I'll sneak around the house and get Gramma."

When Bear returned with his grandmother and Honey, the man was sitting on the trail with his back to them, picking something off his feet. Must be leeches, Bear concluded. The poacher must have entered the pond in an attempt to wash off the smell and red dye. Instead, he was attacked by leeches. Honey and his grandmother moved across the lawn toward the croquet court and hid behind a massive metal sculpture of a great blue heron, ten times bigger than the greatest blue heron ever seen in nature. Meanwhile, Bear signaled to Victor and Zoe that the poacher was on the opposite edge of the property.

Their suspect rose and looked toward the estate before dropping his head in defeat. He moved slowly, shuffling over the sandbags at the edge of the croquet court and nearly tripping on a wicket. After the stumble he paused and looked up again. He appeared to be summoning his strength for the final trek to the house and a shower, a place to hide. Who could know what thoughts were under his hood?

Bear peered through the binoculars. "He's so skinny," he whispered.

When Bear spoke, the suspect turned toward them. Bear and Olivia dropped down behind the stone grill, but not before Bear recognized the figure crossing the croquet court. "It's Floyd Flood," he gasped before clapping his hand over his mouth.

Slowly their heads rose above the edge of the grill. The animal control officer had moved past them. He was approaching the guest cottage on the opposite side of the property. They needed to surround him. When Floyd Flood was on the opposite side of the gigantic heron sculpture, Bear signaled to Victor and Zoe that the poacher was approaching. He acted out directions: 1. Wait. 2. We'll move behind him. 3. When he's close, jump on him. Bear hoped they understood his pantomime routine. It wouldn't do any good to chase Floyd Flood back into the woods. They were fast but they had lost the poacher before.

Bear turned toward his grandmother's position to signal where the poacher was. Honey seemed to think he was calling her and dashed to Olivia and Bear's hiding spot. They were quick to settle the golden retriever behind the grill, but her swishing tail thumped against their legs. Wrapped in the cocoon of his hooded sweatshirt and looking very tired, Floyd Flood shuffled toward Victor and Zoe's hiding spot.

Olivia and Bear dropped onto the patio and counted to twenty slowly, quietly, before peeking around the grill. Floyd Flood's head hung down as he limped toward the guest cottage. They made their move. Running silently, side by side, they formed a barrier behind the poacher: boy, girl, dog flowing effortlessly across the manicured lawn.

When Floyd Flood's right foot stepped off the grass and onto the patio beside the guest cottage, Victor Anaya charged toward him in his soundless wheelchair, followed closely by Zoe in her heavy clomping hiking boots.

At the sight of them, Floyd Flood turned to run back to the woods, but instantly saw Honey the Wonder Dog, Olivia, and Bear. As the poacher took a step backward, away from the children, Honey leapt into the air and knocked

Floyd Flood into the strong arms of Victor Anaya.

"Totally awesome, dudes!" Zoe shouted as she ran forward with a length of rope.

Bear chuckled. He had never seen Honey jump so far. "Gramma, did you see that?"

Sally Parker ran to them from behind the heron sculpture and grinned. She shook her head in disbelief and knelt to hug her dog.

As Victor Anaya restrained the animal control officer, Zoe tied his red-stained hands. When they set him on the ground, Bear noticed his face was equally red. And he stunk.

"What's that smell?" Sally Parker asked, holding her nose.

"Him!" Olivia and Bear laughed before bumping fists, "Kaboom!" and raising their arms high in the air, victorious.

"We caught him red handed," Victor joked, and everyone laughed.

Everyone except Floyd Flood. "You did this to me?" Anger twisted the poacher's words. "I'll—." He slumped back in defeat, unable to think of a threat.

The smell worsened. Everyone in the circle took two steps backward, except Honey. She was attracted to Floyd Flood's fragrance. At first she tried to roll on his legs, but he kicked and flailed in response.

"Get off, you stupid mutt!"

Honey stepped back, sat, and cocked her head. Then she approached him again, but this time it was to sniff his bulging pockets before gently retrieving a baggy filled with hot dog slices.

"That's why she ran to him!" Sally Parker said indignantly. "It was a trick."

Honey trotted away with her find, ate all of the hot dog pieces, and then trotted back to empty Floyd Flood's other pocket.

Olivia was staring at Floyd Flood. "He dropped a burlap bag in the woods…" Her voice trailed off.

"Dude, one of us should get it," Zoe said.

"I think we've got this one." Bear's grandmother gestured toward Floyd Flood, "under control." He was hunched over, barely resembling the blustery man who had written Honey a ticket a few days earlier. "You go, Olivia. Bear can get the police."

Bear ran to the police station, filled with dread. Officer Calvin hadn't taken him seriously before. Why would he now? He might throw Bear out, and then what would they do with Floyd Flood?

Bear tapped on the police station door. It swung open before he could plan his persuasive speech. His brain raced while Officer Calvin stared at him, waiting.

"Come in," the officer said when Bear remained silent. "Come in."

Bear took one step over the threshold and spoke haltingly. "We caught him. We caught the lady's slipper thief." When he wasn't interrupted, Bear took a breath. "We know it's him. We saw him in the woods. Marked him." Bear decided not to explain that part. "We captured him at the Calhoun estate, where he's planted other lady's slippers. We're holding him there now. You have to arrest him." Bear looked at Officer Calvin's stern face and added, "Please."

Bear stepped back against the door frame. "He's a poacher too." He wasn't thinking straight. He should have started with the unmarked traps, out of season, damage to the beaver dams.

Without a plan, he began to argue. "He's a bad person. Killing plants, killing animals. He hurt my grandmother's dog and wrote her a ticket." Bear expected Officer Calvin to disagree with him, but he listened and nodded earnestly.

"Slow down there, champ. I can't help you if I can't understand you."

"Yeah, Floyd Flood. The island animal control officer is a plant thief, a beaver killer, and he tricked my grandmother's dog," Bear stated forcefully. "And he hurt Honey too. She got stuck in one of his traps."

"There's an animal control officer on the island?" Officer Calvin shook his head and reached for his hat.

"Yes! He made my grandmother pay him forty-five dollars because Honey was off her leash. And he used hot dogs to trick her to be bad!"

"They never tell me anything." Officer Calvin looked at Bear. "Come on, I want to meet this animal control officer who hurts animals."

"What's he look like?" the officer asked as they drove to the Calhoun estate with the siren blaring and lights flashing.

"Real skinny. Looks like a scarecrow kind of hunched over. Older than you but younger than my grandmother." Bear paused to think. "He wears a belt and suspenders."

"I know who you mean. That's the Calhouns' new caretaker. He can't be the animal control officer."

Bear sat back in the patrol car and crossed his arms on his chest. "He can be both." Bear smiled when he realized he sounded like Olivia.

Officer Calvin looked at him with a new respect and agreed. "I guess he can."

Floyd Flood must have been working for the Calhouns, Bear realized, digging up lady's slippers for their gardens, killing beavers, and destroying their dams to protect their croquet court from rising water.

"Did you know that there's no legal season for trapping and hunting on the island?" When Bear shook his head, the police officer added, "This time you've brought me a real crime, champ." He gave him a thumbs up. "As for the Calhouns, it could be hard to prove that they're responsible for the damage that's been done. But a little public embarrassment might motivate them to donate money to a worthy island cause."

As soon as Officer Calvin stepped out of his police car he said, "What's that smell?"

"Don't worry, you get used to it after a while," Bear said.

Olivia rushed to meet them. "We have an injured beaver." She tugged on Officer Calvin's sleeve as she spoke, before turning to Bear. "That's what was in the bag." Her voice rose. "He just dropped it on the trail. Just left it."

Victor placed his hand on Olivia's back and spoke to the police officer. "The beaver's paw was injured in a trap. It's scared and might bite, so we're keeping it in the bag. The harbor master's agreed to transport it to Portland. Someone from animal rescue will take over from there. We need you to meet the harbor master at the dock."

"Of course." Officer Calvin removed his jacket and carefully wrapped it around the burlap bag before gently placing the wounded animal on the back seat of his squad car.

But he wasn't taking any chances on his car smelling like a skunk bomb. Floyd Flood was handcuffed and would have to walk to the dock. He was surrounded by Bear, Zoe, Victor, Sally Parker, and Honey, with the police car driving slowly behind them they walked for a mile and a half.

The odd procession received a few curious stares as they passed Mooney's Market, but observers satisfied themselves with the usual island chit chat: "Hi there, Sally."

"Good to see you, Zoe." "Beautiful weather." "Great to have the tourists gone." They pretended that this September parade was a normal occurrence. No questions were shouted, but everyone knew they would be asked about it later. The aisles of Mooney's Market would be buzzing with both plausible and impossible, hilarious explanations.

After the boat pulled away from the dock carrying the poacher and plant thief off the island, everyone walked up the hill to Sally Parker's house. When they turned the corner onto Maple Street, they saw the Professor sitting with Mrs. Frost on her front porch. Olivia and Bear surged ahead, eager to share their news about Floyd Flood and their accomplishments.

But the Professor spoke first. "I have an important update. While I was in the hospital, I had the opportunity to prepare my wildlife presentation and make several phone calls. I phoned the city to complain about the animal control officer and how he treated Honey the Wonder Dog." He paused as Zoe, Victor Anaya, and Sally Parker joined them. "I discovered that Floyd Flood is the Calhouns' new caretaker. They highly recommended him for the part-time animal control position." The Professor looked at them meaningfully.

They responded by laughing, "We know!"

The Professor looked surprised, but continued. "And, Sally was correct. There is no legal season for hunting and trapping on Oxbow Island."

"We know!" they shouted, and then proceeded to tell Mrs. Frost and the Professor all about their exciting day. For once, the Professor was at a loss for words.

17

The warm sun, flickering across his face, woke Bear. He stretched in his bed and felt the aches and pains of the past week's adventures.

"I think my bruises have bruises," he said to Honey the Wonder Dog. She placed her muzzle on Bear's pillow, looking at his face as her tail swished across the wood floor.

Hunger pulled him downstairs. He had been hoping for blueberry pancakes, but the kitchen was clean and empty. On the counter he saw a bowl of cereal and a glass of juice. Beside them was a note from his grandmother. She had gone to Portland to shop, leaving him home alone, without a schedule or assignment. He'd never been alone on Oxbow Island. As he ate his cereal, he wondered what he should do. His parents were coming in a few hours and they were all going to the Professor's lecture on Living with Wildlife at the Seafarers' Museum.

"Honey, what do you want to do?" Bear asked as he rinsed out his cereal bowl. She trotted to the door and looked back at him. "Okay, but we'll stay in the yard." Bear tried to stretch his neck and arms as he followed the golden retriever, but the stiffness that had set in seemed permanent. "I'm too tired to walk in the woods."

Honey raced to a sunny spot in the yard, lay on her side, and fell asleep.

"I think you're tired too." Bear sat beside her and looked out at Maple Street.

It had returned to its usual quiet. That was reassuring, but also made Bear miss his neighbors. In the still morning air he could hear the murmur of the Professor's low voice coming from Viola Frost's house. He must be lecturing Mrs. Frost. She probably loves it, Bear thought. How many times had he heard her say, "Some days I worry the silence will swallow me whole"? Well, she wouldn't have to worry about that for at least a month.

Bear lay back and rested his head on Honey's sunwarmed belly. His head rose and fell with her breathing. As the clouds floated past, he looked for pictures in them, just as he used to do with his grandmother. "I see a lion with a huge fluffy mane," he said to the dog beneath his head. Honey snored in response and her feet fluttered beside him. "Here comes a dragon." Bear closed his eyes and dozed.

A shadow fell over him. He awoke to find his grand-mother, holding several bags from the mall, standing over him.

"Hey there, Buckaroo Bear, your parents are coming on the next boat." At the sound of her voice, Honey jumped up and Bear lost his pillow. "I bought you some dressier clothes. You need to shower and get a comb through that hair." She reached out and tried to tame Bear's unruly curls. "I don't want your parents to think I turned you into a wild woodsman."

Bear liked the sound of that. "Maybe you did."

"No. You deserve all the credit for that. What a week you've had." She swept him into a hug. When she stepped back, she held onto his shoulders and studied him. "I'm so proud of you." Sally Parker brushed his hair out of his face and touched the cut on his chin. "Now, I have things to deliver. It's going to be a busy day. Scoot on inside and shower." She left for Mrs. Frost's with Honey following closely behind.

Bear looked in the bag she had given him. There was a pair of khaki pants, a button-down shirt in his favorite shade of foamy sea green, and a tie. A tie? And it wasn't a clip on.

It hadn't been easy to get his hair under control and he didn't know how to tie a tie. His grandmother was rushing him and fussing about being late to meet the ferry his parents were on, but Bear ran over to Mrs. Frost's with his tie. The Professor sat on the porch in his wheelchair. Instead of the T-shirt and basketball shorts he had worn home from the hospital, he was wearing his favorite jacket, shirt, tie, and flashy track pants with snaps up the sides. His grandmother must have bought those too. It was impossible to get anything else over the cast that covered his leg from thigh to ankle.

"Nice outfit," Bear began. "Can you do my tie?"

"It would be a privilege, Mr. Bear."

Bear knelt beside the Professor's wheelchair. Face to face, he could see each of the twelve stitches in his friend's forehead. The swelling had gone down, but the Professor's usually smooth brown skin was pitted with holes and scratches, all circled by red-and-purple highlighting bruises.

"No offense, but your face just keeps looking worse."

"Your powers of observation are keen." The Professor laughed and straightened Bear's tie. "Go on. You're keeping your grandmother waiting."

They made it to the dock just as Julia and Karl Houtman walked up the ramp. An average-sized person, his mother seemed tiny beside her husband. Karl Houtman was slightly shorter than the Professor but as skinny as an uncooked piece of spaghetti. He had the appearance of a normal man stretched to awkward heights. For most of his life, Bear had hoped he would end up tall like his father, but each passing year had convinced him he was wrong.

At the sight of his parents, Bear waved his arms high above his head and shouted, "Mom! Dad! Over here."

Their faces broke into smiles and they rushed forward.

"You look taller," his father said.

"Really?" Bear hoped his father was right.

"Baby Bear—sorry, just Bear." His mother touched the cut on his chin and grimaced. "You look thinner."

"That's nothing. You should see my bruises—" A poke from his grandmother stopped Bear from saying more

"You've lost your round bear face," his father said as he ruffled Bear's brown curls.

They walked up the hill and his parents peppered him with questions. Bear and his grandmother took turns explaining everything that had happened since he'd arrived eight days earlier. Bear noticed that his grandmother left out the scariest parts. He squeezed her hand when she said, "The Professor had a little accident in the woods. He's making a speedy recovery."

"I can't wait for you to meet my new friends." Bear decided to change the subject before his parents could ask any more questions.

"Do they like comic books too?" his mother asked. "Did you show them your collection? I tried to pack your favorites."

"I don't know." Bear stopped walking and looked at his parents. He had forgotten that his mother had packed his comic books. "You know, I didn't even have time to look at them." They walked in silence as Bear thought about how much had changed in the past week.

When he saw Olivia and Victor Anaya sitting on Mrs. Frost's porch with Zoe, he grabbed his parents' hands and pulled them behind him. "C'mon! You have to meet everyone."

Bear noticed the change in Olivia's appearance first. "Hey, you're not wearing your boots. And you did something to your hair." He wanted to say more but stopped himself. For the first time since he had met her, she looked like a regular kid. A regular kid on the first day of school in all new clothes. It made him a little sad. He had grown to trust the irregular Olivia.

"Your grandmother took me shopping this morning." Her huge smile swept away Bear's sadness. "It's hard for us to get off island and shop. You know." She looked at her dad sitting in his wheelchair wearing a crisp new shirt and tie. "That's why I always wear the same clothes." She reached over and hugged Sally Parker. "Thank you."

"I wanted everyone to look their best. It's an important day."

Bear was relieved to see that Zoe was still wearing one of her bright flowing skirts over a pair of jeans. Some things should not be changed. The Professor's talk must be a lot more important than Bear had thought, since everyone was all dressed up.

Karl and Julia Houtman stood on the lawn, leaning into each other, and watched their son joking and talking with his friends.

"So, this is the Oxbow Island Gang." Karl Houtman grinned. "You don't look very intimidating to me."

"Listen, dude, do not mess with these two." Zoe gestured to Olivia and Bear. "They might look nice now, all cleaned up, but they are totally fierce warriors. Trust me. I have seen them in action."

Olivia and Bear looked away as the adults laughed.

"I have to get Honey and then we all need to hurry to the museum for the Professor's talk." Sally Parker returned with Honey trotting proudly beside her, a large bow the color of lush spring moss, flopping on her collar. "Now we have the whole gang."

Standing on the porch of the Seafarers' Museum, they looked through the windows. Every chair was full except for the front row. That had been reserved for the Oxbow Island Gang. At the back of the room were a reporter and cameraman from the local television station, along with more people. Dressed up in suits and fancy clothes, they had to be from off island. Olivia and Bear looked at each other and raised their eyebrows in surprise. Half the island was sitting in the museum. Bear had never imagined that so many people would want to be lectured by the Professor. Honey entered the room first, followed by Victor and the Professor. The crowd began clapping. By the time they were all seated in the front row, everyone else in the room was standing and cheering.

A well-dressed woman in high heels click-clacked her way to the front of the room and the crowd quieted.

"Who's that?" Bear whispered to his grandmother.

"Governor Chase."

"That's the governor!" Bear whispered to Olivia.

"Our governor?" Olivia's eyes were wide and round. "Maine's governor is here?"

Bear could only nod and turn to face the elegant silver-haired woman who had begun to speak.

"A week ago, my dear friend Malcolm Yeats called me and informed me that his friend—" she looked directly at Bear. "You're a young man with many names. What should I call you?"

Bear ducked his head and looked at his friends. "Buckaroo Bear" made him smile when his grandmother called him that. Most of his friends called him "Bear," except for Mrs. Frost, who always called him "Berend." He saw his mother standing in the doorway, holding his father's hand and brimming with pride. She had called him "Baby Bear." But he always stood a little taller when the Professor called him "Mr. Bear." It seemed to be a formal occasion, so why not?

"You can call me Mr. Bear," he answered in his most mature voice. Olivia gave a nod of approval.

The governor continued without pausing, "Malcolm told me that Mr. Bear had discovered an environmental threat on precious Oxbow Island. An individual was disturbing the fragile lady's slipper, illegally trapping, and destroying beaver habitat. Mr. Bear was determined to catch this individual and protect your island. Over the course of the past week Mr. Bear and his friends, the Oxbow Island Gang, succeeded in not only identifying the person responsible for this destructive behavior, but they captured him, had him arrested and removed from the island.

"It was not easy. They persevered, overcame challenges, and endured serious injuries. Because of their heroism and commitment to the environment, I am here to present them with the Rachel Carson Award for Environmental Stewardship, along with our profound gratitude." She held up a mahogany plaque with gilded lettering for the audience to see.

"Please, come up and join me." Governor Chase gestured for Bear and his friends to join her at the podium.

Honey immediately jumped up and trotted toward the Governor. She held her tail high, her long golden fur waving like a flag. The crowd burst into laughter at the sight of the golden retriever with the large green bow adorning her collar.

Sally Parker and the Professor beamed at the stunned faces of Zoe, Bear, Victor, and Olivia.

"C'mon, Buckaroo Bear, don't be shy," his grandmother whispered.

The rest of the Oxbow Island Gang tugged on their new clothes and self-consciously followed Honey to the front of the room. Bear scanned the audience of smiling faces as they posed for pictures with Governor Chase and their plaques. There were people he had never seen before and they were all clapping.

"I have two more announcements," the governor said when everyone had returned to their seats. "The beaver you saved is recovering at the Maine Wildlife Park. Her front paw was severely injured by the trap. She can't be released back into the wild, but they will take care of her. She has her own pond and lots of branches to chew on. You should go and visit." The governor looked directly at Bear and Olivia before continuing. "Also, in honor of your efforts to protect the island's wildlife and its ecosystems, an anonymous donor has given five thousand dollars to improve the woodland trails. This money will be used to clear trails, repair bridges, and make the trails more accessible for people with disabilities."

Olivia and Bear turned to each other and whispered, "the Calhouns! Kaboom!" They bumped fists.

The Professor's lecture was more interesting than Bear had expected. Was it because Bear had become so attached to the island's patches of wilderness? Or had he gotten better at understanding his friend's way of talking? Either way, it was encouraging to see so many people interested in protecting plants and wildlife on their island.

After the awards and lecture, everyone was invited to the Anayas' for a potluck picnic. It looked like a parade as the large group of islanders walked down the middle of Water Street to the Anaya home with Victor and the Professor leading the way. Zoe had offered to give them a ride in the taxi but they had declined. They planned to have a wheelchair race from the Goofy Gull Gift Shop to the gas station. The idea delighted Mrs. Frost, who suggested that the taxi could be the lead car, making sure the road was clear ahead of the racers. Everyone laughed. The next ferry wouldn't be there for thirty minutes. There was no traffic. Still, Mrs. Frost climbed into the taxi and the matter was settled.

Victor and the Professor removed their ties and handed them to Sally Parker along with their plaques. They rolled up their sleeves. Olivia and Bear marked the starting point and the islanders lined the street.

"On your mark," Olivia yelled with one arm in the air.

"Get set," Bear continued and raised his arm.

"Go!" they shouted in unison and dropped their arms to their sides.

From the moment the wheelchairs crossed the start line it was obvious that Victor's years of experience in a wheelchair made it an uneven match. Within seconds he was twenty feet ahead of the Professor. Victor tipped his chair back and rolled along on his back wheels. The Professor, awestruck, stopped moving and gawked. The yelling crowd snapped him out of his reverie and urged him forward. He began rolling again. The Professor caught up just as Victor began turning in tight circles on his two back wheels. As the Professor pulled ahead, Victor began rolling in reverse. And that was how they crossed the finish line, side by side, the Professor facing forward and Victor facing backwards.

Bear and Olivia ran down the street toward the finish line. Both men had impressed and surprised Bear. When he congratulated them, it was obvious that the race had been an exhausting test for the Professor and a fun demonstration for Victor.

"It's a lot harder than he makes it look," the Professor gasped.

As people expressed their surprise and admiration for Victor's athleticism, he was quick to point out that it was the Professor who was recovering from major surgery and should be congratulated. With that in mind, Bear pushed his friend the rest of the way to the Anayas'. The Professor slumped back in his seat, grinning.

As the island residents flowed into Victor Anaya's yard, he sat in his wheelchair beside the vegetable garden, watched, and smiled. Olivia bustled around, showing people how to use the apple cider press, getting plates and cups for everyone, arranging food on the picnic table. Bear got a chair for Mrs. Frost in the shade next to the Professor and brought them each a plate of food. Sally Parker moved through the crowd, introducing her daughter and son-in-law to other islanders. Bear visited with his friends after he brought them each a glass of cider, but he kept looking over at Victor, who sat alone, quiet, subdued.

As people gathered around to sign the Professor's cast, Bear drifted away from the joking crowd to check on Victor.

"You okay?"

"Yes." Victor rolled back and forth slowly. "Just taking it all in." Without looking at Bear, he said, "It's been a long time since we had something to celebrate." After a moment he spoke to his hands, which were folded in his lap. "I've been imprisoned by my pride."

Bear hoped Victor wasn't going to start talking like the Professor. It was bad enough having one friend he could barely understand. "Well, I think you have a lot to be proud of. You can juggle and sing and I've never seen anyone race a wheelchair the way you do."

Victor looked up and smiled at Bear. "Pride can be bad too. I was too proud to let my friends see me this way." His hands rubbed the wheels of his wheelchair.

"Your wheelchair?" Bear didn't understand Victor. "But, that's like your super power." When Victor didn't respond, Bear continued, "I was embarrassed about hanging out with girls. That's why I got in a fight with my friend. Is that pride?"

Victor looked as confused as Bear felt. Victor shook his head and grinned at Bear. "You do know that Olivia is a girl, right?"

"Yeah, but she's my friend." As the words left Bear's mouth, he realized that Jasmine and Devi were his friends too.

He sat on the raised garden bed beside Victor and watched the party. Victor and Olivia had spent six years shut off from their friends and neighbors. Was Victor thinking about what they had missed? Or was he quietly enjoying this moment?

"Do you think Zoe brought her guitar?" Victor asked.

Bear jumped up and raced to the taxi. She always had it with her. If she started playing, then Victor would sing and joke and the celebration would be complete.

Walking back across the lawn with her guitar, Bear scanned the crowd, looking for Zoe. Then he saw her, walking beside Victor toward his guests. She must have noticed Victor and been concerned too. Bear's grandmother was right. Zoe was a lovely person.

Mike Mooney stood on the picnic bench, hollering for the crowd to gather around him. The guests quieted and moved into a tight circle of neighbors, friends, islanders. Mike Mooney raised his glass of apple cider high in the air. "I would like to drink a toast to the Oxbow Island Gang for their crime fighting efforts..."

Bear Houtman felt his chest filling with a warm glow.

"...and for bringing us all together today to celebrate. It's wonderful to be back at the home of my good friend Victor Anaya." Tears slipped down the husky grocer's cheeks as he looked at his old friend. "It's been too long. I've missed you."

As the men hugged, Bear turned to Olivia. "I can't believe I have to leave tomorrow."

"Tomorrow?" Olivia spoke slowly. She began picking up discarded paper plates and cups. "I was thinking I might go back to school too."

It was Bear's turn to look surprised. "Really?"

"It's not like Dad needs me." She smiled and turned toward the sound of her father and Zoe preparing to entertain the crowd.

"You don't have to go to school to learn stuff."

Olivia stopped tidying up, tilted her head, and narrowed her eyes as she stared at Bear. Of course that would be obvious to her. She hadn't been in school for six years and she was almost as smart as the Professor.

"I just meant that I learned a lot this week." Bear threw a stack of paper plates in the trash bag Olivia was holding. "I learned that I'm wrong about people most of the time. I didn't know how tough the Professor was." Bear walked around the picnic table to pick up napkins that had blown into the yard. "I thought your dad was handicapped, but he can do anything." Bear dropped the napkins in the trash bag. "And I was wrong about Officer Calvin. He's okay." Bear gestured to the police officer singing along with Zoe and Victor.

Olivia chuckled. "All that time in the woods and now you understand people?"

"Yup." Bear smiled. "I was wrong about you and I think I was even wrong about me." Olivia looked puzzled. "I thought I would hate it but I really liked jumping off the dock and…" he struggled for another example. "I don't even care if people call me Baby Bear anymore."

Olivia nodded knowingly. "When will you be back?"

"My parents said I can come for Halloween."

"Really?" Her face lit up. "Oxbow Island is the best for Halloween. Wait and see. We'll have a blast."

Acknowledgments

A huge thank you to my first readers Eileen Lee, Mary Anderson and Kathi Conley for their encouragement and feedback. Stephanie Fullam, my earliest reader, has supported me through every phase of my writing career.

The trained editing eyes of Ali Mayeda, Melissa Kim and Ruth Butler were essential in strengthening the story line and characters.

Hugs and kisses to my grandsons Barrett and Mika for inspiring me to write a story about the transformative power of a loving community.

Now put down this book and run outdoors to explore and play!